THE GHOSTS OF GALWAY

KEN BRUEN

A Mysterious Press book
for Head of Zeus

First published in the US in 2017 by Mysterious Press,
an imprint of Grove/Atlantic, New York

First published in the UK in 2017 by Head of Zeus Ltd

9 7 5 3 1 2 4 6 8

A catalogue record for this book is available from the British Library.

ISBN (HB): 9781786697004
ISBN (TPB): 9781786697011
ISBN (E): 9781786696991

Printed and bound in Germany by CPI Books GmbH

Head of Zeus Ltd
First Floor East
5–8 Hardwick Street
London EC1R 4RG

WWW.HEADOFZEUS.COM

For

Des and Gerry Bruen

The respectable branch of the clan

and

For

James Casserly

and

My beloved brother-in-law

Mark (PJ) Kennedy.

Plus Eva Devin.

These extraordinary people

Gave extraordinary light to our respective lives.

The bed of heaven to you three.

Peadar Ryan, extraordinary guard.

Over and over I had been replaying a conversation with my

Once friend,

Former ally,

Now bitter enemy

Sergeant Ridge.

Not for the first time, I was in a very dark place. A failed attempt at suicide, a deadly diagnosis on my health, and the continuing forward March of Trump.

I figured I would mend some fences, try to get my friendship with Ridge back on track.

And I mean if your health is fucked, surely your friends/enemies might cut you some slack.

Right?

Nope.

I phoned Ridge. The doctor had gotten in touch with me again and implied that maybe . . . just perhaps . . .

His diagnosis was off the mark a tad.

Now did I go and tear his fucking head off?

Or

Buy him a crate of Jameson?

No. I rolled the dice and stayed hopeful.

Ridge was curt on the phone, a real cold cunt.

Because I was tired, in every area that weariness can touch, I asked to meet her.

Met her in Garavans and, completely out of character, she ordered a large vodka, slimline tonic. I went with the Jay. She was dressed in a soft green sweater; you might even stretch and suggest: emerald? White jeans that dazzled in their brightness but there the shine ended.

She looked fatigued.

Well, fucked actually.

I said,

"You look terrific."

Got the stare.

She said,

"This Emily, nothing about her is kosher."

(Emily/Emerald/Em, a psycho punk storm of murderous intent who had taken a weird shine to me and was a continuous thorn in Ridge's sense of justice.)

I laughed, mimicked,

"Kosher? Seriously? From a West of Ireland woman?"

She slammed her glass on the table, her very empty glass, said,

"One way or another, I will get her, and if you are any part of that it will be a joy to do you too."

I considered telling her my fifty/fifty chance of being out of the game. Would I get a break, some sympathy, maybe even a shot at repairing our tattered friendship?

I said,

"I have not been feeling well."

She was on her feet, spittle leaking from her mouth. She fumed,

"Well? Are you kidding me? You haven't been well for twenty years and what on earth are you telling me for?"

I tried,

"Because of our, um, you know, history?"

She gave a short bitter laugh, moved to the door, then, as parting,

"You could die tomorrow, I could give a fucking toss."

I sat completely still, then muttered,

"All in all, I think it went okay."

Later, a tinker woman I gave a few euros to asked me,

"Do you believe in ghosts?"

I said,

"Only the ones provided by Jameson."

She chided me.

"Don't mock. Ghosts are swirling all 'round you and soon will flood your life."

PART 1

"A dog when injured
crawls off to an isolated place
lies low until the wounds, if not healed,
at least covered over."

A failed suicide is a sad, sad fucker.

The final chapter of Alvarez's *The Savage God*, perhaps the best account of suicide, details the author's own attempt at the desperate act.

For me, the years of fuckups, pain, mutilation, grievous loss would, you think,

. . . Lead to wisdom?

Like fuck.

Led me

To

A

Job as a security guard.

Suicide by boredom.

If I was to continue aboveground, I needed money. My last outing, adventure, case left me not only spiritually bereft but broke.

The ad for security guards sought those with a military background or police force experience. Some fancy dancing with my CV and I actually looked if not respectable at least not outright criminal.

The guy who interviewed me said,

"If you can walk and don't have an outstanding warrant you're in."

My first assignment was protecting a warehouse on the docks. I had a torch and phone which, I guess, if thieves attacked, I could resort to foul language. Mostly the job was dull but that suited me just fine as I had more than enough action in past years to satisfy the most jaded adrenalized junkie. Plus, I could read and be paid for doing so. The ideal job. A guy I knew back from the States who had worked security in New York and who was armed told me,

"Jesus Jack, first I thought, *gifted.* I need never fear assholes no more, but then I'd get home and play the sad whining music, you know, the *why did she leave me dirge* stuff? *They give you a free razor blade when you purchase it.* Then I'd get depressed and want to kill myself and had the gun in my lap!

"But what if I missed? And was lying wounded for days?"

The first month, I was on nights and liking it, no need to talk to anyone, I was all out of conversation. Clocking out the Friday, end of my shift, a supervisor was waiting and said,

"Taylor."

I nodded and he said,

"The head honcho wants you to meet him."

"Why?"

He shrugged, said,

"No idea. He only this week went through the employee files and seeing your name asked for you."

"Who is he?"

He took a deep breath, then,

"Alexander Knox-Keaton, from some, somewhere in Ukraine."

Ukraine!

With all the waves of migrants literally throwing themselves into the ocean to flee Syria and other deadly regimes, Ukraine seemed to have momentarily dropped from the headlines, but it was nice to know one of their people was living it large.

I said,

"Not exactly your expected Ukraine name. I'd have expected something more

. . . Slavic?"

He sneered.

"Fucking get you, Mr. Knowledge. Shame you are wasted on this piss poor excuse of a job."

I didn't rise to the bait. Oddly, since my failed suicide, I felt less inclined to kick the living shit out of assholes.

He said,

"Here is his address and you are to report to his *mansion* tomorrow at noon."

I echoed,

"Mansion?"

He gave me the look, the one that cries,

"Dumb shit"

Said,

"You will see and be sure to wear a suit."

"I only have my funeral one."

He sneered.

"Might well be just that."

"They spent the afternoon butchering horses."

(Matthew McBride, *A Swollen Red Sun*)

Early on the morning of October 1 a reveler, staggering home, went,

"What the fuck?"

He was standing or rather swaying at the top of Eyre Square. If he had been of a literary bent,

He might have intoned,

"Doth mine eyes deceive me?"

But being hungover and a moron, he uttered,

"WTF."

In the middle of the square was the body of a horse. A bright chestnut already showing extreme rigor mortis. The drunk added,

"In all me born days . . ."

He moved down to take a closer look but a sudden spasm doubled him and he projected a line of vomit that would cause CSI all kinds of headaches. He wiped his brow and swore,

"That is my last drink. Ever."

He didn't of course stop drinking but he did avoid Eyre Square for a long time. He also stopped backing horses.

I dressed to, if not impress, then to make a statement. That being,

"I'm fucked."

So my now very battered Garda all-weather coat, scuffed Doc Martens, a once white T now in shades of washed gray, and my fade to faded 501s.

The man from Ukraine had his mansion near the golf links. I had as a child worked as a caddy, thus ensuring a lifetime aversion to the sport.

I let his name swirl in my mouth to get a sense of it.

Alexander

Knox-

Keaton

No way was this his real name but I could care less. His house was a glass affair, screaming two things:

Money.

Bad taste.

A car, BMW, with two occupants, either bodyguards or the local cops. Which, depending how much juice you had, could be both.

I stopped to survey the house and, with Galway Bay at my back, let out a deep sigh. I was bone tired, tired of assholes and stupid money. I lit one of my now five a day rationed cigs and blew the smoke toward the monstrosity of glass. Then muttered,

"Let's rock and moan."

Headed for the door. Opened as I reached it, a young Filipino woman in maid's uniform said,

"Mr. Taylor?"

I nodded and she stepped aside to let me by.

In the hallway was a huge tapestry of what appeared to be a page from *The Book of Kells*.

The maid led me to a study, ablaze with books, the walls lined with beautifully covered volumes and they had that look of being well used. Not for show then. But that rarity. A working library. Thick heavy wooden furniture that you might imagine carved from a line of oaks but, too, seemed to be lived in. An open fireplace had a raging inferno going on.

Few things as comforting as that. Like an echo of the childhood you only ever read about. The maid withdrew and I examined the books up close, nearly missed hearing the door open behind me, turned to see a man who reflected the grandeur and solidity of the room. A man over six feet tall and power oozing from every pore. He was wearing a tweed suit, very Anglo-Irish of the '50s, and, I shit thee not, a cravat, adding a slight P. G. Wodehouse vibe. He had a full head of well-darkened hair and a face that testified to the use of money and force. His age was a well-preserved seventy or a very fucked forty.

He held out a big hand, calloused and creased so not just a sightseer. Boomed,

"Mr. Taylor."

I took his hand and was relieved he wasn't one of those bone-crushing idiots who think that means anything other than

"Bollocks."

I said,

"Jack, please."

He smiled, revealing one gold tooth among the very best cosmetic dentistry. He said,

"And I am Alex."

Then,

"Sit, sit and let me treat you to a shot of Slain whiskey."

Made at Slain castle and promoted by Lord Henry Mount Charles himself and not due to hit the market until late 2017.

Was I impressed?

Yeah, a little.

Taking a heavy tumbler of Galway crystal, I sank into an armchair. Inhaled a smoky whiff of the drink. Fucking marvelous. He asked,

"How are you finding the job?"

Tell the truth or kiss arse?

I said,

"Has me bored shitless."

He laughed, seemed actually amused. Then he asked,

"*The Red Book*, this is known to you?"

His English had that tight careful air of the second-language perfectionist. Almost a clipped precision and you nearly hear the translation occur. I said,

"Apart from Mao's little red one, no."

He topped up our glasses and then,

"You are, I believe, an . . ."

He paused to taste, savor, the next word,

. . . *Aficionado*

A conniver of books?

Conniver?

I said,

"I like to read but a bibliophile? Hardly."

He liked that word, could see him store it. He continued,

"*The Book of Kells*. This you know?"

"Know is hardly the description but, yeah, I've heard of it."

He settled himself into the chair opposite me, composing some lecture he'd prepared.

Began,

"It was written around AD 800. It is a book of the Gospels. No one knows who wrote it but it is believed to be a series of monks."

He paused.

I said,

"So?"

He gave what can only be described as a wolverine smile, said,

"A rival book came out shortly after, decrying the Gospels, and is generally regarded as the first true work of heresy."

Let me digest that, then.

"Known as *The Red Book*, the Church of course denies its existence. It is sometimes known by its title in Irish but, alas, that pronunciation is a little beyond me."

I supplied,

"*An Leabhar Dearg.*"

He was impressed, said,

"I am impressed."

I said,

"Fascinating as this little side trip down a Dan Brown alley is, what has it got to do with me?"

"I want you to get the book."

I stood up, said,

"Thanks for the drink and the chat."

He said,

"Here."

Offering a check it seemed like. Well, fuck it. I am always going to look at one of those suckers.

Gasped.

Went,

"You are shitting me."

He said,

"I am told you are dogged in your dedication to a case and that, somehow or other, you get results."

This was patently untrue.

But was I going to argue? A gift horse is what you throw a saddle on and shut the fuck up.

He continued.

"You are familiar with the term *rogue priest*?"

I nearly laughed, wanted to ask,

"Nowadays, is there any other kind?"

But went with,

"Indeed."

"The curator of sacred manuscripts and other treasures in the Vatican recently died and his assistant, a Father Frank Miller, took the opportunity to not only quit his vocation but also abscond with *The Red Book*."

If he was expecting a comment, I didn't have one. He continued.

"Mr. Miller is now hiding out in Galway and has offered the book for sale."

I said,

"So buy it."

He sighed.

"Would it were so easy but Miller is, as they say, *gun shy*."

This term would come back to haunt him.

"I want you to negotiate with him."

I said,

"I don't really do well with priests."

"Ex-priest."

"Whatever. I am sure you have better people to deal with him. I am quite likely to end up beating the shit out of him."

He laughed, delighted, said,

"This is exactly what is required, fear and loathing."

What the hell. I could give it a shot.

I said,

"Frank Miller. Shares a name with the renowned author, graphic artist, moviemaker."

He looked as if this was of no relevance. I added,

"The film was *Sin City*. Nice serendipity, don't you think?"

He didn't.

Said,

"Just get the job done."

Heard the steel in there and wanted to tell him to go

. . . Fuck his own self.

But the check.

Won out.

Said,

"I'll get right on it."

My dog Storm seemed to know I had recently considered suicide and was now keeping a canine watchful eye on me. In the apartment, he'd sit on my chair, staring at me as if to ask,

"What's up, bud?"

I said,

Going American,

"Phew, I nearly bought the farm there, pal."

He didn't speak U.S. so just wagged his tail. I grabbed the leash and got a short bark of utter joy. Shucking into my Garda all-weather coat we headed out, my pockets holding treats and a small flask of Jay. Ending October, the air was dry and alive, people shouted *how yah,* and the warm vibe was largely a result of our soccer team beating the Germans by a goal.

Beating the best.

With a government hell-bent on eroding the will of the country with a continuation of the hated water tax, it was good to have a reason to smile. We headed for the Salthill promenade and I relished the little dog's sheer unadulterated joy in the walk. The dead horse in Eyre Square was a hot topic and especially since a notice had been sent to the papers with just this:

"FADH."

Speculation on it being a shortened form of an Irish word led nowhere. It seemed obvious that it stood for

. . . *flogging a dead horse.*

Or was that just too facile?

Set a priest to catch a priest. Father Malachy was my dead mother's pet, a practice back then of pious ladies adopting a tame cleric and having him in tow to demonstrate their holiness. My mother was one mean, wicked bitch and that she had this idiot in thrall spoke volumes as to the characters of them both. He loathed me, agreed with my mother's description of me

. . . *as a useless drunk.*

Our paths continued to cross. One memorable time I even saved his arse from serious allegations of indecency. Was he grateful?

Was he fuck!

He was the most determined smoker on the planet. No electronic capers for him. Despite all sorts of upheavals, he managed to cling to the shreds of his parish. Just a prayer ahead of the lynch mob. I hadn't been to Bohermore for a time and had near forgotten the warmth and goodness of a real neighborhood. I stopped at a new off license, bought a bottle of Paddy. Malachy was truly old school in his whiskey. A man in a flat cap, donkey jacket, his nose beet red from booze hailed me with,

"Jesus, Taylor, you're alive."

A new corruption of language was the young people answering any question with

Basically.

They used it without rhyme or reason. I looked at the man, said,

"Basically."

St. Patrick's Church was the parish I grew up in, back in the days when the church ruled. Now it was simply a small church with smaller aspirations. I went to the house beside it, knocked, waited. Door opened by a housekeeper in her very battered fifties and with a scowl that was set in the '40s.

"What?"

She barked.

"Good morning, my dear,"

I tried.

Phew-oh.

Good was not an adjective she had ever met and seemed unlikely to adopt now. I added,

"May I see the parish priest?"

"No."

Terse but concise.

She went to close the door, but my boot prevented that. She near spat.

"What is that?"

Staring at my foot.

In a very polite voice, I near whispered,

"That, darlin', is my shoe, which I shall put so far up your arse you will scream hallellaia or such like."

"You . . .

You're not right in the head."

No argument there and I did the thing that freaks the very best of them.

I smiled.

Father Malachy looked fierce. In both senses of the word, angry and fucked. A wreath of smoke hung like bad news above his head. He snarled,

"Taylor."

Warmth.

I handed over the bottle of Paddy and, without even looking at it, he put it in a drawer. I asked,

"We're not having a drink?"

He lit a cig, blew smoke at me, said,

"'Tis drink has you in the state you're in."

So, business as usual.

I said,

"You might be of some help to me."

He laughed with no hint of humor, plain bitterness, said,

"What's in it for me?"

Christ.

I said,

"Clerical satisfaction."

He looked like he might spit, said,

"Whoever sold you that lie is a Protestant."

The worst insult in priestly lore. I persisted.

"I was thinking of putting some euros to the roof fund. He smiled, said,

"Now we're talking."

Handed over a few notes and they joined the bottle in the drawer. He gritted,

"What do you want?"

"A priest, ex actually, named Frank Miller."

Right on cue, he said,

"*Sin City.*"

How could he know that?

I asked,

"How could you know that?"

He made the *humph* sound, said,

"I have Amazon Prime."

I shook my head. Life still had surprises. He added,

"I'm a big Mickey Rourke fan."

Saw my jaw drop, said,

"There's many say I have the look of him."

For fuck's sake.

I asked,

"After the plastic surgery fiascos?"

He ground the cig on the floor. I understood why the housekeeper was like a demon. Then,

"Call me in a day and I'll see what I can find."

I tired.

"Thanks."

He said,

"May need some more cash."

I sighed.

"The roof?"

He sneered.

"Nothing wrong with the roof, it's solid, like the papacy."

I was leaving when he said,

"You had some kind of Goth girl in tow, a heathen I hear?"

Emily.

I said,

"You're well informed."

He waved a dismissive hand, said,

"People think I have some interest in you because I knew your sainted mother. I don't."

No reply to this.

He added, almost like he'd near forgotten,

"The girl, someone kicked fifty kinds of murder out of her."

"What?"

He stared at me, said,

"You're not deaf."

Well, kind of, actually.

He eased a bit, maybe seeing the shock in my face, said,

"She's in the hospital. Bad state I hear."

As I was heading out the door I nearly ran into the housekeeper, who said,

"Good riddance to bad rubbish."

Jesus, people actually said that kind of thing?

I looked back, shouted.

"God love you."

"*The Red Book* wasn't so much a repudiation to the Gospels but a challenge to the Church to deny its existence."

(Father Frank Miller)

Emily

Em

Emerald

A Goth-like crazed girl who had blasted into my life two years ago and left me

Bewildered

Burned

Bewitched.

She may or may not have been involved in the deaths

Of

Her father

Mother

Various lowlife.

And managed to mangle and massacre my heart and mind. She woke in the morning and chose a personality for the day. Usually a personality bordering on the maniac. Whatever else, it was hard to ignore her. True too. She had saved my life and hide in many ways. Her act was to disappear for long stretches then blast back with utter impact. She was a long sentence from beautiful but her sheer vitality was highly addictive. There was a tiny defect in her left eye that seemed to deepen the emerald effect. Well, a deeply flawed stone but valuable nevertheless.

Was she

Bipolar

Byronic

Or simply a blip on the mental calendar?

Fuck knows. But boring? Never.

She had by many circuitous routes and canny connivance the ability to conjure up a constant cash flow.

And she liked to spend.

Recklessly.

I was relieved when she left and exhilarated when she returned. She had given me the gift of my dog Storm. And if you like people who love dogs, then she was a shoo-in.

But I have learned some things in my bewildered career and that was to know how extremely dangerous she was.

She had that aura that read

"*Fuck with me at your peril.*"

Emily was at NUIG hospital. I stopped to buy some grapes and the guy in the shop said,

"Of wrath?"

I said,

"Little early for literary smart arses."

The National rugby team had defeated France in a stunning display of courage and grit, then gone to Cardiff to lose to Argentina.

Fuck it.

Prior to the match, hotel owners in Cardiff had increased their rates by almost 100 percent. Echoing the Irish government in their thinking: if it moves, price it to death.

Em was in ICU and thus not allowed visitors. Standing outside was Bean NI Iomaire, Sergeant Ridge. Once a great friend but now a cross between an enemy and an ally but a very precarious ally. Since the death of our mutual friend Stewart, she had become outright hostile. I tried,

"Comas ata tu?"

(How are you?)

She scoffed.

"Your attempt at Irish is like your friendship."

Pause.

"Woesome."

I reached out my hand, said,

"But good to see you, Ridge."

She slapped my hand away, said,

"Your girlfriend is in a bad way."

Fuck.

I said,

"She is not my *girlfriend.*"

Ridge smiled, not with any warmth but with a mean edge, said,

"Of course, you don't *do* friends."

I gave up, asked,

"Any notion of what happened to her?"

"Yes, she did what she does best, pissed someone off. In this case, the wrong person, apparently."

"Got any person of interest?"

She didn't even deign to answer, just smirked and strode off in that Garda way of

"*Fuck you, civilian!*"

Did I care?

Only a wee bit.

I managed to grab a doctor, tell him I was an uncle. He did the doctor gig of telling me,

"We will have to wait and see."

Which was very closely related to Ridge's response if somewhat more refined.

As I passed Ridge on my way out, I handed the grapes to her. She was caught, dare I say, *off Guard*, and asked,

"What do I do with these?"

I said,

"Thing is, they're slightly bitter so just add them to your reservoir."

I hit the pubs, not drinking but asking about the assault on Em. Took a while and I very nearly said,

"Aw, fuck this."

But persisted,

And

In the Kings Head, a guy asked,

"Is there a few quid in this?"

There was.

And got,

Em had been giving it large the previous night and an apprentice thug named Corley had made a pass. She had very loudly dissed him and he waited outside . . . with a baseball bat.

He was apparently a minor dealer in GHB, the new form of deadly ecstasy that was hitting the streets. Some further inquiries to ensure he was not deeply connected. I didn't want to step on some kingpin's runner but, no, he was a bottom feeder. He liked to hang out near the Claddagh Basin and throw rocks at the swans. An all-round winner.

I went home, took the dog for a joyous run in Eyre Square. A number of people attempted to rub or chat to him but he was having none of it. He gave that canine look of

"*I already got family.*"

Worked for me.

Home to set out his dinner and water, then took down my holdall and shoved my hurley in there. Had still some coke from a previous encounter so did some lines to get cranked.

Be doped to beat a dope.

At the basin the sky was clear blue, a pretense of good weather that fooled nobody; we knew shit was coming and called it winter.

Wasn't hard to find young Corley. You heard him before you saw him, one of those yahoos who shout at passing old people.

I got a good look at him. Built like a rugby player but a lot of flab in there and, from his movements, you knew he let his appearance do his intimidation; it was bulk without strength. He suffered, too, from that huge disadvantage of never receiving a serious puck in the mouth. That makes you not only vulnerable but downright careless. I put the holdall down and took out the hurley, gave it a trial swing, and got that reassuring *whoosh*. All good to go. He had noticed me now and his small ferret eyes told him,

"Victim."

Told him wrong.

He said,

"Bit old for that, aren't you?"

I gave him my best smile, asked,

"You want to try it?"

Held out the handle of the hurley to him. Something in my manner alerted the serpent in him to be wary but his overriding arrogance couldn't discern a threat. He reached for it, said,

"Stupid old fuck."

As he took the handle I pushed with all my might and it rammed into his stomach. He staggered back, managed,

"What the fuck?"

I said in the same even tone,

"Oh, did I startle you?"

Stood back, whistled, then said,

"What is it you kids say? *My bad*?"

Then pushed forward, driving him back, and he lost his balance, tumbled into the water. I went to the edge and swung again, catching him on the side of the head. I said,

"Now that is a score that the referee will not contest."

An elderly man who had been on the receiving end of the idiot's shouting, gave me a beatific smile, said,

"I'm not sure that young . . ."

Pause.

"*Man* can swim."

Looked over at the fool in the water who was obviously struggling then added,

"Let me amend that. I sincerely hope he cannot swim."

Father M called that evening and gave me the address of the rogue priest.

I said,

"Thank you."

And got,

"Don't bloody thank me, pay me."

The blessings of the priesthood are a mystery to behold.

I told the pup about the thug I put in the water and, by the way he wagged his tail, I think he approved.

I watched *Everest* and was suitably impressed by Jason Clarke as Rob Hall. I ate some Irish stew with a tiny hint of Jay added and gave the pup some in his dish. He preferred a hint of

Smithwick's in his. When the storm hit on the mountain, he hid under the sofa, and if there had been room I might have joined him.

Frank Miller, the rogue priest, was staying in a hotel on Dominic Street, one of those new anonymous buildings that allowed short-term stays. And didn't require a whole lot of ID. Money did the talking. There was a reception desk with a hostile guy reading a book, *Spanish for Dummies*. He had the book up high to discourage inquiries.

I was not discouraged, greeted,

"Hola, señor."

He was not amused. I said,

"Basic greetings are at the very beginning of the book."

He put the book aside and looked like he might punch me, snarled,

"What do you want, asshole?"

I said,

"Little manners would be good."

I produced a wad of notes, said,

"Donde esta Frank Miller."

He hesitated and I laid the notes on the counter, said,

"Mucho dinero."

He grabbed them, said,

"Room 201."

Up shabby stairs then knocked on 201. It opened almost immediately. Not sure what I was expecting, probably a whiskey refugee and old.

Neither.

Young guy, in his early thirties, long brown hair, bland face, dressed in gray tracksuit. Then I was falling backward from a punch. He was about to follow through with a kick but I grabbed that and flipped him, then, getting up, I dragged him by his hair into the room, kicked the door shut, said,

"Stay down or I will break your fucking neck."

The introductions out of the way, I looked round the room.

Bare.

Thomas Merton would have been comfortable with it. I asked,

"Where is the book?"

Up close he didn't seem as young though maybe being dragged by the hair ages you. He picked himself up, slowly, watching my boots carefully, asked,

"Are you working for the Church?"

I nearly laughed but went,

"I represent the private sector."

He measured me, definitely found me wanting, but decided further tussle was wasted. Said,

"The book is gone."

So I did what you do with a stubborn priest. I walloped him.

Twice.

Once to get his attention and the second because it plain felt good. He staggered back, moaned.

"I think you broke my nose."

I said,

"Oh, it's broken, all right. I can tell by the tilt but, you know, gives a touch of character to what is, let's face it, a weak face."

I swear, he nearly smiled but the pain in his face told him this was not wise. He said,

"From your accent and your whole black Irish face, you are probably Catholic. Didn't they teach you it's a sin to touch a priest?"

I laughed, said,

"Whoa, the clergy and touch? You really want to go there? Plus, the new teaching is that it's a sin *not* to touch a priest."

I gestured for him to stand and he moved to a hard back chair, settled with a sigh, said,

"There is no book. There were remnants of a manuscript but I burned it."

I said,

"Now, that is not going to fly, padre. Why would you burn it if you went to the trouble of stealing it?"

He gave me the look that says,

"*Lord, give me patience.*"

Said,

"I was a high flier in the Vatican and the likes of you . . ."

Here, he gave me a look of such disdain,

Continued,

"Couldn't even begin to imagine the power I had."

I let the sheer arrogance of that hover, then,

"*Had* is the operative word. Now you are just a punk hiding out in a third-rate hotel."

He nearly spat, said,

"You know nothing, you are . . . *nothing*."

I said,

"Know this. There is a very powerful man who wants the book and I am, let's say, *the good cop*."

He wasn't buying this, said,

"Run back to your employer and tell him to forget the whole thing."

I stood, said,

"I could wallop you some more and, in truth, I would be glad to do so but I'll pass along your message and,"

I headed for the door, added,

"May God have mercy on your soul."

If this was supposed to intimidate him he hid it well.

"The red in *The Red Book*
Is a tomato color. Made from red lead.
The color lies on the top of the vellum
And in some cases,
Through old age, wear and tear,
Tiny pieces have flaked off
Leaving an impression of rough handling.
Despite the fading over the time
The red still has the power to impress."

(Father Frank Miller)

A few months back, I had been given a deadly medical diagnosis. Then, like so many cases in the country, they found it was mistaken and urged me to be reexamined.

Like,

Fucking right!

The governor calls and you get off death row, you're going to go back, and ask,

"Please, may I have my death cell back?"

The Health Department was paying out small fortunes in compensation and the minister on TV daily saying,

"We deeply regret."

Not a person in the whole country who believed the *regret* bit. You hear of people who get a second chance who proclaim,

"I could smell the roses."

As the kids go,

"Like, *really*?"

In truth, Jameson never smelled so compelling.

A morning in late October, I was in Crowes in Bohermore, and telling Ollie, the owner, about the misdiagnosis. He went the very Irish route of

"Well, you look well on it."

The double *well* implies they couldn't really give a fuck . . . but appearances' sake. A guy on the stool next to me, reading the *Daily Mirror*, said,

"You should sue."

The new Irish pastime:

Litigation.

He was reading the sports section and added,

"Ferguson has a new book out."

I nodded. Ferguson's autobiography was the bestselling book in Ireland followed by *One Direction*, and I was interested, asked,

"More about Man U?"

He shook his head in disgust, said,

"It's about how to succeed in life."

We all shook our heads in unison, thinking Fergie had gone American.

Happens, even to the gifted. He said,

"Says that the two most powerful words in the English language are . . ."

Waited.

Ollie said,

"Love you."

I tried,

"Pay me!"

He said,

"Well done."

I finished my drink, headed out, was near assaulted by a woman collecting for a basketball court for the youth of Salthill.

Jesus wept.

With refugees dying in the ocean every day and the number of homeless reaching shocking proportions, we needed the Salthill yuppies to have a basketball court?

She said,

"Anything would be of great benefit."

I gave her my most earnest look, which is part compassion and most ways menace, leaned in, said,

"Well done."

The following morning, a dead sheep was left on Eyre Sq. This time they left a note, or rather a large placard with this:

HFAS

Everybody seemed to get this meaning.

Hanged

For

A

Sheep

The dead horse had evoked horrors, the poor sheep less so. People were now just curious and indeed intrigued. It was generally agreed that it was some antigovernment protest. And just about anything that stuck it to them bastards was approved by most of the country. Our political leader claimed he sat on a bench with a homeless person and . . .

Get this!

He spoke to the poor bastard for all of twenty minutes.

And to think they gave a Nobel Prize to that deadbeat Gandhi.

The All Blacks defeated the Wallabies in a crushing match and Mourinho was due to be fired from Chelsea. After Liverpool fired the great Brendan Rodgers, it was open season on all, especially sheep.

The culprits certainly had balls. A large van was seen at the end of the square, backed up on the grass and in no apparent rush, then they flung open the back doors and dumped the animal, then, again with no haste, drove back into traffic and disappeared.

Were there witnesses?

Were there fuck!

Hundreds.

And thus a hundred descriptions.

The Guards said, with conviction if little certainty, that a definite line of inquiry was being followed.

Right.

They were looking for a truck in a city with twenty thousand registered vehicles alone.

I could imagine Ridge's face

—and relieved I wouldn't be seeing her for a while.

I was wrong about that of course.

"The ellipsis is used to trail off in an intriguing manner."

"After surviving the trenches
I now find myself
With the horrors of peace."

(Jack Taylor, senior)

I didn't realize it but I was about to get hold of a dream, albeit a mad one, but still . . . I do believe that a dream, however insane, will get you out of bed on many a dire cold wet November morning.

My neighbor Doc was slowly renewing his friendship with me. We had fallen out over Em and it was nasty and British. Like life.

I liked him a lot, principally because he had a great affection for the pup. He was English but kept that subdued. He had served with some distinction and darkness with the British army and he sure kept that tight wrapped. This was still the Republican West of Ireland no matter how far we might have traveled since the Peace Initiative.

We shared a love of fine whiskey

Bad whiskey

And box sets.

Too, he read voraciously and, like me, in a sort of controlled fever. Meaning he would follow a theme like say true crime, then read all and everything on that. Vinny from Charlie Byrne's bookshop was on his speed dial. In his varied career, what most impressed me was his attempt with his army buddies on Everest. They had turned back at Hillary Step. Just below the death zone.

This resonated in me in so many ways that it was almost preordained. Currently he had lent me

Into Thin Air by Jon Krakauer,

The Death Zone by Matt Dickinson,

No Way Down by Graham Bowley.

And probably my favorite, Matt Hail's account of the 1996 disaster.

In addition he had given me a copy of *The Summit*, the Oscar-nominated documentary about the K2 tragedy. To watch eleven climbers die on the screen and the heroic Irish guy Ger McDonnell, who died trying to save the Korean team members. So, smitten with mountain fever I surely was.

The mind-set of the Sherpas echoed the way the Irish had once been before Celtic Tigers, crushing financial reparations, and water bills killed our very spirit.

Doc told me his last attempt on Everest brought down many of his team with HAMF.

High-altitude mountain fever.

What resonated with me most was Doc saying,

"On the mountain, more people are killed on the descent than the ascent."

Story of my life right there.

Getting high was mostly a soaring ride of exhilaration and expectation then

The coming down

Hell.

He explained that the fever was a result of a swelling of the brain and caused the climber to imagine things, lose focus, stagger 'round dangerously. Again, I had a whole lot of experience with that. Then he surprised me with,

"I am planning one last attempt and this time I am traveling light, a two-man team, to hit it fast and furious."

He paused, then,

"If I fail, then being buried is not the worst way to go."

And

Gave

Me

My

Dream.

Ghosts are, supposedly, silent.

I was telling the pup about my hope of traveling to Everest. He was eating his breakfast, some spareribs from the stew of the evening before. I told him about the various attempts on the mountain but he seemed singularly unimpressed. Then his head went up and to the side. I was having a visitor. Sure enough, a loud bang at the door.

I was just getting up to answer when a further series of loud wallops hit the door, I shouted,

"Jesus, have a bit of fucking patience, I'm coming and it better be important."

Ridge.

With a young Guard in tow who had that formless look that Saturday nights on the beat would beat the fuck out of fast. She marched in and the pup growled. The young guy demanded,

"Is that animal aggressive?"

I gave him my, dare I say, *guarded* smile, said,

"It is not the dog who bites."

Could be wrong but did Ridge allow a tiny flicker of a smile. He blustered,

"I must inform you sir that you are threatening a Garda Síchoána in the course of his or her duty."

Ridgc snapped.

"Ah, shut up you emit."

I did wonder what an emit was?

Then turned to me, demanded,

"Do you know an individual named Frank Miller?"

I did what you do.

I asked,

"Why?"

The emit said,

"We'll ask the questions."

Jesus, seriously!

I said,

And do admit that I have waited many TV years for this, I said,

"I refuse to answer on the grounds I might incriminate my own self."

The dog wagged his tail so I was amusing at least one. Ridge said,

"For fuck's sake, Taylor."

She sounded her wit's end. I said,

"I met him one time."

She consulted her notebook and I thought,

God be with the days I had one of those. She asked,

"Where were you between the hours of eight and midnight yesterday?"

I made a show of concentrating just to fuck with her a little more, then,

"Drunk in Fahy's bar in Bohermore."

She raised her eyes to heaven but found no solace there, said,

"You might need to contact a lawyer."

"Why?"

"Mr. Miller was found dead and we know from a hotel receptionist that you were his last visitor."

"How did he die?"

"Violently."

God almighty.

As she left, she said,

"Looks like you are screwed this time, Taylor."

The young guy glared at me, said,

"I am looking forward to having you down the station."

I gave him a caring smile, said,

"Go with God, my son."

Later that day, I met with one of the few remaining Guards who would talk to me. Owen Daglish.

We met in Naughton's on Quay Street, now a hubbub of hen and stag parties. I remembered when this was a dead street with nothing but a pawnshop. Owen looked seriously hungover, as he had done for the past ten years. Not so much one episode but the very box set of hangovers. He said,

"I'm dying here, Jack."

He had the serious cure, double hot whiskey and pint chaser, a heated boilermaker, if you will. I stayed on the cold Jay. Never ceases me to observe the *cure* occur. Owen gulped down the toddy, exclaiming,

Oh, sweet Jesus, let it stay down.

No.

Oops.

Fuck.

Yes, maybe.

And then it hit, his face got the glow, the sweat evaporated, the shakes disappeared, he sat up straight, looking for fight, as they say. He literally sprang from the stool, urged,

"Come on, cig time."

Definitely on the mend if you want a cig. Outside it was cold and we huddled like lepers with the other wretched smokers but with a defiant air of camaraderie.

Owen lit a Major, the serious nicotine route, drew in some lethal amount, then on the exhale said,

"I had to go to the wall on this request of yours, Jack."

Meaning it would cost me.

Dear.

I handed him a wad of notes and, for a moment, seemed he might count it. Caught my look and put it fast in his jacket, said,

"This is a bad business mate. That poor bastard Miller? Whoever did for him, it was vicious, beat the poor whore for a time before killing him, shoved pages of a book in his mouth so forcibly that it crushed his tongue."

I felt a shiver, asked,

"A book?"

Back inside, he signaled for a refill, the cure coursing through his system and, of course, screaming for more. Then,

"Yeah, some pages in, get this, *Latin*!"

Oh, fuck.

Before I could ask, he added,

"A priest translated it."

"Whoa, what was a priest doing at a crime scene?"

He gave me a look of

"Yah dumb fuck."

Said,

"He was still alive for a time and the priest was called for the last rites."

He got the fresh drink, said slyly,

"Translation costs extra."

I reached for more cash, slid it across with bad grace, thinking,

Hope it chokes you.

He tried to chill the situation. Said,

"Next round is on me, pal."

Nervous though.

I snarled,

"The translation?"

"Oh, right, I have it written down."

A crumpled piece of paper, then a big show of getting his reading glasses, then read,

"Hic est diabolized."

Waited.

I near spat.

"The fuck does that mean?"

He waited a beat, then,

"He is demonized."

Woodrow Wilson said, “The hyphen is un-American.”

(Note the hyphen required in “un–American.”)

Fleur de peau
Sensitive to anything that touches his skin

Time to go and see my boss. He would not be too thrilled that I failed to procure *The Red Book*. The fact that Frank Miller was dead and apparently with pages of said tome shoved down his throat. Would it cut any ice?

Would it fuck.

From my previous meeting with the great man, I knew he only understood results. Plus, I hadn't shown up for the security job, figuring I was already working on something for him. I asked Doc to mind the pup while I was thus engaged. Doc was busy in preparation for Everest. I hadn't yet asked him if I could come along.

I mean,

Here I was,

A drunk,

Xanax popping,

Two fingers mutilated,

A limp,

A hearing aid,

Dodgy health prognosis,

Recent wanna-be suicide.

Who wouldn't want to climb the highest mountain with me? He had in his time summited

K2.

Annapurna.

McKinley.

Kilimanjaro.

Failed to reach the top of the North Face of the Eiger. I asked,

"You picked your team yet for the climb?"

He looked fit after a few difficult months and the mountain enterprise seemed to have rejuvenated him. He said,

"My old sergeant was first choice but he got a job as security consultant in Iraq so he's out."

Then he added,

"You are tied on a short rope to a guy on the most dangerous terrain on the planet, you need to know he's the guy."

I nearly said,

Better than a short fuse.

But for once my smart mouth did the right thing and shut the fuck up. I ventured,

"You know if you need a person to keep track of the provisions, like a manager at base camp, I could handle that."

He stared at me for a moment then burst out laughing, managed,

"You!"

He was truly shocked, said,

"You can hardly climb the stairs."

I was now late to meet with my boss and a rage was beginning to leak all over my being. I said,

"I don't think I'm that bad."

He nodded, said,

"You're right. In fact you are way worse."

Now he was shaking his head with the sheer incredulity of it. I said,

"You know what? Go fuck yourself."

I strode off, the pup in tow, and he shouted,

"Jack, don't you want to leave the dog with me?"

I threw back,

"I'd rather drown him."

So, okay, a tad petulant, not to mention . . . *the drama.*

Sister Maeve, one of my few remaining friends. A nun as scarce ally, go figure. I had helped her in a small way many years before but she seemed to place a huge debt of gratitude to me. Was I going to dissuade her?

Was I fuck?

She was like the point man for her convent. She lived in the outside world and managed the lines of communication between the enclosed community and life. They chose the right front person. She exuded a warmth that was as natural as it was rare. She dressed in gray and one touch of color, a silk scarf I had given her. She lived in a small house on St. Frances Lane. But a decade of the rosary from the Abbey Church. I didn't go empty-handed, stopped off at McCambridge's to get goodies. She opened the door, greeted me with a tight hug, and the pup was delighted to see her. I handed over the clutch of goodies and she said,

"Oh, you didn't need to do that, Mr. Taylor."

"Jack."

I left the pup with her and, several hours late, headed off to report to

Alexander

Knox

-

Keaton.

Yet again I marveled at the sheer impressiveness of that name. Name like that, it was preordained you'd be CEO material. Dish washing wasn't really in the cards.

I was ushered into his office with no fanfare, just glares of cold hostility from his bodyguards. I was anticipating him being

Angry

Aggressive

Sarcastic

But

Scared?

Never.

He was scared now.

Very.

His type, they do the scaring. Being scared is not ever on their radar. He had a haunted look, and he kept darting his eyes toward the window. He barely acknowledged me, reached in his desk, tossed an envelope on the counter, said,

"Your severance pay."

I decided to play dumb,

Asked,

"For which job? The security or *The Red Book*?"

Fuck, did I hit a nerve. He literally jumped, said,

"Take your money and go, Mr. Taylor, I don't expect to be seeing you again."

And on cue one of the bouncers/bodyguard appeared behind me.

Of all the troubles in my troubling life, I have never been troubled with minding my own business.

Never.

I asked,

"The poor bastard Miller? With pages of a book rammed down his clerical throat? Do I just forget about him?"

My arm was grabbed and I feinted to the left, came down hard on the instep of the guy's foot with my Doc Marten, then swirled 'round and sucker punched him in the throat with an open flat hand.

He went down like the proverbial sack of spuds. A.K.K. Sighed, said,

"You are buying in to a world of hurt."

Sounding not unlike a cut-rate Schwarzenegger and reached for his phone. I turned to leave and threw,

"Be seeing you, buddy."

And got out of there fast before the rest of the crew arrived.

I stopped up the road and bent over, gasping for breath, muttered,

"Went well, all in all."

"Did you put sugar in?"

He liked two spoons.

She had. Then, as we sat, she said,

"Mr. Taylor."

I mentally said,

Jack!

She continued.

"I think you have many times in your life wished to travel the high road but circumstances led you to the lower plain."

No argument there. Then,

"I think you have a good strong heart but life seems more acceptable if you adopt a shell of, um . . ."

She searched for a word that wouldn't cause offense, then,

"Hardness."

She poured the tea and then buttered the bread. I said,

"Out there"—and vaguely indicated the window—"there is precious little softness and any sign of weakness . . . they will annihilate you."

She blessed herself which is, I suppose, answer enough.

She gave me a deep searching look, then asked,

"Do you believe in forgiveness?"

Aw, fuck.

I near snarled.

"I believe in retribution."

She was upset, tried,

"The most difficult act of all is to forgive oneself."

I tried not to snigger, said,

"Isn't that God's job description?"

She was flustered, torn between trying to explain and giving me some scant comfort.

A fool's errand.

I mentioned the horrendous massacre of concertgoers by terrorists in Paris. Then added for pure maliciousness,

"Never thought I would quote Putin but he said if the terrorists see their mission is to get into heaven, it's my mission to send them there."

Horrified her, as was meant.

The pup sunk under a chair; tension freaked him. She made one last valiant attempt, said that old hackneyed justification

"God's ways are mysterious to behold."

I stood up, gave a low whistle for the pup, attached the leash, gave her a brief hug, parted with

"Oh, there is no mystery, sister. He likes to mind fuck."

I regret the f-word but, fuck, I do not regret the sentiment.

Not one fucking bit.

I had read enough of James Lee Burke to nearly see his
Ghosts
in
the
Confederate
Mist.

Those days as I trudged through the streets of the city, on corners, at the tips of alleys, on the canal waterways, on bridges in the slight distance, around the cornices of churches, amidst crowds lining up for early shopping bargains at T.J. Maxx, slipping through the back doors of back street pubs, in the young people who gathered on the grass at Eyre Square, I saw
My
Very
Own
Ghosts
of
Galway.

My parents, one loved and one despised.

Oh, so many of my friends:

Stewart, the most decent person I'd ever encountered.

A treacherous close friend whom I lured to his death in the Claddagh Basin and never regretted it for one moment. He was evil behind a smirk.

And, weird as it sounds, more priests than a minor scandal.

Too, a gorgeous child, Serena Day, who haunted me every day.

Phew-oh.

A life indeed less ordinary and littered with those I deep mourned and those psychos even deeper despised.

I had lived a small life in a small town with smaller aspirations and yet managed to create havoc and chaos under the guise of assistance.

An echo of the Vatican, really.

I let out a considered breath and watched it dance among the shattered dreams. If there is a meaning to life in the concept of *having made some little difference*, then I had wrought bedlam and decay.

As Padraig Pearse wrote

And
I
Went
Along
My
Way

Pause.

Sorrowful.

"The existence of *The Red Book* was perpetuated by the Church as a sinister scare tactic to keep outspoken priests in line."

(Frank Miller, ex-priest)

I was watching the new Marvel series

Jessica Jones.

Netflix had a huge critical and commercial success with *Daredevil.*

This was the second of a planned four-part series.

Phew-oh. It was amazing, stunning, and moving in equal measure, especially to a guy like me who knew fuck to nothing about comics.

A ring at the door, the pup barked. I switched off the iPad. Took a deep breath, just knowing it was bound to be more shite. A young guy, punk hairstyle, battered combats, an even more worn combat jacket, with a smile and expectant manner.

I snapped,

"What do you want?"

His smile broadened. He asked in a semi-posh accent,

"Might you be Mr. Jack Taylor?"

The pup was low growling, his small head down in the attack mode. The guy said,

"I'm not good with dogs."

I waited.

Then,

"Oh, right, Emily sent me."

Then he smiled some more. I asked,

"Was there a message?"

He considered this, then reached in his jacket and both the pup and I went to alert. He pulled a book out of his jacket, said,

"Here."

It was bound in red leather and for a mad moment I thought,

The Red Book?

Looked at the title.

Don Quixote.

He said,

"You're welcome."

I was baffled, asked,

"Why, does she think I'm Don Quixote?"

He laughed, said,

"She said more like Sancho Panza."

There was no sign of him leaving, I asked,

"Something else?"

Again with the smile, he said,

"I'm waiting to be invited in."

Now I smiled, with absolute no warmth, said,

"Never happen son."

He put out his hand, said,

"I'm Hayden, that is with a capital H."

The pup had decided he was no threat, just an idiot, and went back into the apartment. I said,

"Time to fuck off, H."

He lost the smile, edge leaking over the mouth, said,

"Emily said you could be . . . difficult."

I said,

"Indeed, and you know what?"

He wasn't entirely sure this was a question so settled for the ubiquitous,

"Okay?"

The tone rising up like a blend of whine and question. Another vocal our young had adopted from the U.S. I said,

"You need to fuck off with a capital F."

He said,

"I was hoping to like, you know, hang with you and, like, you know, chill."

I let out a sigh and decided it was wasted energy. He was definitely the type who had never been punched in the mouth or, at least, not often enough. I said,

"The dog doesn't like you."

Now he let the whine full play, whined,

"Like seriously? Is that even a reason?"

I shut the door with

"The only reason that counts."

The pup wagged his tail. It seemed I still had some moves.

On Eyre Square, a dead cow was found with white paint on its flanks reading

"Not cowed."

The papers yet again had a wild old time with speculation as to the culprits.

Were they

Water protesters,

Pranksters,

Supporting the nurses,

Animal rights,

Or simply

Pissed off?

Like the whole country.

Superintendent Clancy made a forceful statement with the usual blather,

"*Definite line of inquiry.*"

Which meant they had zilch. The culprits were definitely getting our attention but to what?

I opened *Don Quixote* and was rewarded with the aroma of fine leather and gold binding, a scent of class. I didn't expect to find a clue in there but what the hell, tilting at windmills seemed like as good an idea as any others.

Next time I went to the hospital I was allowed to see Emily. She was out of Intensive Care and had a private room. Our health service was in such a shambles that most patients had to lie on trollies in corridors before they even caught a glimpse of a doctor. Only Em could have gotten a room. She was sitting up, dressed in a bright kimono-type top, her face heavily bruised and bandages around her head. The eyes, phew, they burned even more fierce than ever. She snarled,

"The fuck kept you, Taylor?"

I said,

"Life, I guess."

She studied me, then,

"You're old, Jack."

Great, just fucking great. I asked,

"How are you?"

Got the withering look, then,

"I'm hurting Jack, in so many ways, but hey, I have the key to recovery."

"Determination?"

She scoffed.

"Drugs, heavy-duty ones."

I tried,

"I dealt with the guy who hurt you."

Was I expecting gratitude?

A little.

She sneered.

"He was just one of the disposable ones."

Did she mean it literally or was she getting philosophical? I asked,

"What does that mean?"

She said,

"The ghosts of Galway."

A tiny shudder crossed my spine and lodged. It was like she could read my mind but I asked,

"Who?"

She adjusted her position then reached in the nightstand and took out an e-cig, flicked it, blew large clouds of vapor, said,

"Same dudes who are dropping animals in Eyre Square."

I thought that was ridiculous, said,

"That is ridiculous."

She settled down in the bed, some of the bluster gone, then,

"They are a combination of Old Testament, ferocity, fundamentalism, and your plain run-of-the-mill violence."

I wasn't buying this, asked,

"Why?"

"They want to return to the Latin Mass, parental authority, the Ireland of the fifties. No fun, just bleakness and darkness."

I said,

"Like an Irish ISIS."

She said,

"Pretty much."

A thought hit and I asked,

"How come you know so much about them?"

She smiled in a knowing way, said,

"I was fucking their head honcho."

Like most everything she said, it was designed to shock. Finding the truth among her chaos was a challenge. I didn't feel like traveling that mad road again. I said, sarcasm leaking all over my tone,

"How nice for you."

She said,

"You don't believe me."

I asked in all sincerity,

"Does it matter?"

She looked like she might leap from the bed, spat,

"It is going to be a little difficult to help me if you think I'm making it up."

I could engage a bit, asked,

"What is it you think I or *we* can do?"

She eased back in the bed, let out a long sigh, conceded,

"You might not be up to it after all."

Here's the crazy thing, my pride took a wee hit, and I asked,

"Why?"

She turned to the wall, said very quietly,

"It's not just you're old. You're weak."

I wish she was the type you could give a reassuring hug to. Fuck, I wish I was the type who could give one. I said,

"We might work something out."

I didn't catch her quiet reply and moved closer. She said,

"Fuck off."

I was standing outside the hospital, debating a pint in the River Inn. A car pulled up, a blue Toyota, the window rolled down to reveal Ridge. She was dressed in casual clothes, her hair tied back in a severe bun, accentuating her *no nonsense* air. She said,

"Get in."

I was in no mood for any more shite so asked,

"You asking or ordering?"

She sighed, sounding not unlike my dead mother, a walking bitch. She gritted her teeth, said,

"A request."

I got in, made a show of settling my own self. She pulled off with a screech of tires. We drove in silence until she asked,

"How is the she-wolf?"

"You mean Emily?"

Gritted teeth, then,

"Yes."

"She is recovering and good of you to care."

She near rear-ended a lorry, then,

"I don't care."

Well, that killed that topic. I played fake pleasant, asked,

"Day off?"

"Crime doesn't have days off."

I laughed, genuinely amused. Asked,

"They teach you that in detective school?"

She pulled up in Woodquay and parked, very badly, mostly from bad temper. I suggested,

"I could show you a real simple method of effortless parking."

Nope.

She went,

"The day I need you to teach me anything I will shoot myself."

She got out, indicated the Goal Post, asked,

"Have you been there?"

One of the very few pubs I'd missed, I said I had not. Followed her in and she grabbed a table at the rear, barman came over, asked,

"Get you folks?"

She said,

"Two coffees."

The guy smiled, then,

"And you, Jack?"

"Pint and chaser."

She glared at us both, then to the guy,

"That will be just one coffee."

He gave her a sympathetic smile, said,

"Oh, I think I realized that, *officer*."

She rounded on me.

"You said you hadn't been here and how does he know to call me officer?"

I said with world-weariness,

"Ah, Ridge, so many questions and so precious little time."

She intensified her glare.

I said,

"I have not been here but I do know my bar guys and bar guys know their cops."

The drinks came, and if the coffee was meant to revive it didn't. I asked,

"What's on your mind, Ridge?"

She considered her options, then,

"There are rumors of a gang of antiestablishment who intend to cause chaos in the city. They have some daft name like *spooks*."

"Ghosts,"

I said.

Surprised her. She had not been expecting a result so fast, asked,

"You know them?"

Tiny hint of admiration. I said,

"Heard of them, an urban rumor, supposedly they are the ones dumping animals on the square."

She had to ease out the next question, hating it.

"Would you let me know of anything else you hear?"

"Why? Why would I help you, Ridge?"

She had no idea but tried,

"Once a Guard?"

Here was an opportunity for some serious payback, for all the years of cold abuse I could simply tell her to go fuck herself. I wanted to, for the instant bullet adrenalized rush of that.

I said,

"On one condition."

She looked dubious, asked,

"What?"

I gave her my very warmest smile, almost meant it, said,

"You have to be nice to me."

She looked like she might throw up, said,

"Not really sure I could do that."

I let that simmer, then,

"I'm kidding, you could no more be nice than me joining the priesthood."

She managed,

"Thank you, I think."

I asked,

"Do we hug now?"

Ghost Number One

Jeremy Cooper was what used to be termed a *spoilt priest.* It didn't mean petulant, though there were certainly enough of those about. It was that he had left the priesthood early because of circumstances.

These ranged from

Women

Greed

Arrogance

Or all of the above.

Jeremy left simply because he couldn't take direction or *orders* as he read them. Born to lead was how he saw it and the Church did not. A high flier in the Vatican was the very least he had expected. Got a dud parish in darkest Sussex. Uh-oh.

No way.

Reared in London to Irish parents, he was immersed and enamored in all things Celtic. Not the new Ireland but a mythical subdued island where the clergy ruled. He was tall, athletic, played hurling with a viciousness that let his built-up frustrations bleed. He had even features that somehow failed to jell and gave the impression of not being quite finished. Brown eyes that misled to an impression of kindness. He had never been troubled by that weakness. He discovered he had a talent for crooked bookkeeping and used that to set up a *financial consultancy* first in Dublin and then in Galway.

Galway sang to him. It still had a whiff of republicanism and the Celtic Twilight still glimmered.

There was an atmosphere of unrest that cried out for a strong hand. That would be him. He believed in Ron Hubbard's dictum that

"If you want to make a million, make a church."

He wanted to make a massive change so he would make a city. Followers. Essential to get foot soldiers and where better than the ranks of the disenchanted, the chronically unemployed?

A hatchet man.

Vital.

Terry Wood, known as *Woody.* A former insurgent, as they were now so PC-termed. He had been at a loss since the peace initiative. If he ever had a CV it would list

Thug

Psycho

Maniac

And all-round brute. It wasn't so much that he embraced violence—he loved it, was never more alive than beating the hell out of somebody. He looked like a small gorilla and knew it. He met JC at a prayer rally. The best venue to find the crazy and the seekers. He was in the midst of kicking a young guy who had bumped into him when he felt his drawn fist held. Turned to see JC who said,

"Would you like to be rich and famous?"

His initial response of

"Fuck you, asshole"

Didn't emerge, instead,

"Tell me more."

So it began, the ghosts began to take substance.

JC asked Woody,

"Can you get a dead horse?"

Woody, not noted for his humor, nearly said,

"I have flogged some."

But knew enough about his leader to keep it serious. He did try,

"Easy to get a live one and just . . ."

Pause.

"You know, shoot the fucker."

Got the look from JC, who commanded,

"What do we believe about obscenities?"

Woody thought,

We fucking avoid them.

Said,

"It debases those who resort to them."

JC appreciated the value of a man like Woody. A guy who seemed to thrive on what the Americans nicely term *black ops.* The down-and-dirty suite that was so necessary to get a movement off the ground. Woody was the personification of the shit sandwich principle. Pat their head while you kicked their arse. Convince a guy like Woody that only you fully appreciated his unique talents and bolster that fragmented ego, you had a pit bull of undying loyalty. Feed him a crazy notion and then the trick was to let him believe he had thought of it. Plus, there was the added rush of utter mind fucking.

Money.

Hit the rich guys, butter them up with titles they would hold in the new organization, then find their weakness and exploit the hell out of it. It was a hit-and-miss affair at best. The death of the Celtic Tiger made the new money guys cautious but, persuade them that they would be part of the new ruling junta, they bought in.

Blackmail with a velvet touch.

He had it blacklined in his book of *ghosts*. The journal he was keeping with a view to publication after he was famous. All the greats did that. Made him smile to consider a

Ghostwriter.

Mainly he was a humor-free zone but did appreciate irony if it was delivered with a hammer and intent.

But for serious cash it was hard to beat the old reliables. Women and theft. Combine both. He did.

Julia Finch, an old bird like her very name. She came from old-time money and was old-time with it, that is, mean. He wooed her as if he meant it. Gave her the codswallop she wanted to hear. Too, played on that old adage of *bad boy*. Well, even more alluring to an Irish woman, bad priest.

Sin

Sacrilege

Sex.

Irresistible.

But fuck, he earned it. Big time. The woman droned on

And on.

While he had to act like he was rapt. Thinking he wanted to wrap his hands 'round her neck. Once she had signed most everything to him, JC asked Woody,

"How do you feel about Julia?"

Woody was wary; was it a trick?

He tried,

"She seems very devout."

He wanted to add *sir* but it stuck in his throat. JC said,

"She says you put your hands on her."

He was speechless. JC gave a rueful smile, said,

"I don't believe even you are *quite* that desperate."

Woody knew he was being deeply insulted but wasn't sure why, knew enough to know that, when you are cornered, a shot of pious shite might work, said,

"We all have a cross to carry."

He didn't believe that for an instant, else why did God give the world au pairs? JC was shaking his head, as if more grief was coming.

It was.

He said,

"She says you are a vile, treacherous, thieving piece of garbage."

Phew, he had to bite down. JC was watching him closely, said,

"Speak freely."

He knew he would have to avoid cursing and to tread lightly, spat,

"Cunt."

How do you track a ghost?

Lightly.

That's what I did. Innocent questions thrown in to pub conversations, not a driving interrogation but a soft gentle inquiry. Nothing at first but slowly a trace began to emerge.

Unemployed men suddenly having a cause, a purpose. Hints of a new movement that would once and for all deal with the crooked bankers, the sleazy shot callers who had robbed the country blind.

Oh, and the water charges.

Any organization that promised to end the hated tax was a winner. A few times I saw a small burly man buying rounds for everybody. His name I learned was Woody. A Friday evening I managed to maneuver myself next to him at the bar. He was shouting for a large round, I said,

"Great. Make mine a double."

He was not amused, did that slow turn of someone who anticipates violence, asked,

"I know you, fuckhead?"

My mind clicked to delight. I was in a mood to pound on a thug, said,

"Whoa, no need for that, I thought you were some rich ejit buying for everyone."

He gauged me, then,

"You thought wrong."

And went back to ordering the drinks. I grabbed his arm and he went into fight mode. I said,

"Not rich? Just an ejit, then?"

He clenched his face and before I could prepare I was pulled from behind, a voice saying,

"Let's go."

And was dragged away by Hayden!

Hayden?

I said,

"You've got to be kidding me!"

He looked even younger than the last time I saw him. He said,

"Emily told me to watch out for you."

I was exasperated, asked,

"*You,* you are going to *protect* me?"

He smiled, said,

"I have some moves."

Jesus.

I said,

"Try this one: fuck off."

He smiled and I wanted to punch his lights out. He said,

"How about if I told you I had *The Red Book*."

WTF.

I went,

"You?"

"Like I said, some moves."

I only half believed him but, if he hung with Emily, anything was possible. I asked,

"So can I see it?"

He began to turn away, said,

"Not so fast Jack-o. You have to earn that."

And he was gone before I could grab him.

On Eyre Square, a van pulled up, threw open the doors, and left a clutch of dead swans on the grass. A mother with a young infant gasped, then fainted. A crowd gathered and the overwhelming response was

"Dirty bastards."

Before, with the cow, horse, a certain sick humor might have been derived, but in Galway there is no humor concerning the swans. They are as sacred as something can be in a city that insists on honoring writers not from the city. Anyone but natives, being the credo.

Superintendent Clancy was beyond rage, gave Sergeant Ridge the

Rant of a decade.

The newspapers went ballistic, crying for Clancy to resign. Like that would happen.

There were many witnesses, describing everyone from

Refugees

Nonnationals

Students

Water protesters.

Then storm Desmond hit and the swans were forgotten as the city was blinded, blasted, and battered. Overnight it was estimated the cleanup would cost twenty million euros. Plus, the EU had decreed we owed close to a billion for not conserving energy. The people were so exhausted with bills, taxes, and levies, the general feeling was

"*The check is in the mail, assholes.*"

In the midst of chaos there is always a level of utter ridiculousness, which went to the Water Authority, which, in addition to sending out bills, sent everyone who registered with it a bonus of a hundred euros whether they had paid their water bill or not. One man wrote to the papers asking,

"If the U.S. doesn't want Trump, could we have him?"

Almost as an aside, the sacking of Mourinho by Chelsea went largely ignored. Rory McIlroy bought a 50,000 euro engagement ring for his newest financée and it was generally asked,

"But did he pay the water charges?"

Ghost

of a Chance

Might

be Jack's definition of happiness.

My neighbor Doc was finalizing his plans for an attempt to climb Everest. His plans did not include me. I ran into him as the pup and I returned from a walk. In a moment of madness, I had volunteered my services for the trip.

Right.

Me, a sodden drunk with mutilated fingers. A hearing aid, a limp, an on/off affair with prescription pills. Just the ticket for Everest. I asked,

"You give any thought to me tagging along on the adventure?"

He bent down to rub the pup's ear, then,

"You were serious?"

Fuck.

I said,

"I may not be in the best of condition."

He gave one of those short laughs, immersed in bitterness, snapped,

"And what exactly could you bring to the table?"

. . . bring to the table?

For fuck's sake.

I said,

"Attitude?"

He brushed past me, said,

"Try sobering up first."

Phew-oh.

Such assholes I had to consider friends. Because most all I knew were in the graveyard. Outliving your enemies may be noteworthy but your friends? It is sadness on wheels.

I said,

"What's the bug up your arse?"

He shook his head in that manner of

Lord, give me patience with fools.

He said,

"When I first met you, your drinking was almost fun and I admit I did enjoy some *sessions* with you, but when it is 24/7 it wears a little thin."

Fuck me pink.

I wanted to get my hurly and beat him six ways to Bloody Sunday, but maybe it wasn't too late to earn some air miles with God, so I went,

"Go with God, my friend."

He muttered something garbled and left. The pup looked at me and I swear he seemed to say,

"Another one bites the dust."

Christmas came and one miserable affair it was. Storms and violent wind and that was just the politics. Emily was released from the hospital and promptly disappeared. She did send me a gift. *The complete Tom Russell album collection.*

With a terse note:

"Sing as if you wanted to."

Plus a check for a serious amount, note pinned on it:

"I stole this."

Probably.

I laid low, lots of box sets, treats for the pup and fifty-year-old Jameson. The highlight was a small brilliant concert by Johnny Duhan. I was being careful, kind of, with my health. The previous scare had made me very conscious of time. The city half expected reindeer to be thrown on Eyre Square but the perpetrators had decided to take a break from leaving dead animals there.

The new year brought the death of Lemmy and then David Bowie. Could there be a worse way to begin the wretched year?

I had been to the doctor and got told,

"You are somewhat of a miracle!"

The fuck is that?

I asked,

"Meaning?"

The doctor did that peering at me over the rim of his glasses, the look that sees nothing, absolutely nothing worth saving. He said,

"Last year, you seemed . . ."

He searched for a term that didn't include litigation.

Got,

"You seemed very weak."

Then he peered some more at a chart, probably his golf scores, and said that jingle they live by,

"We would like to do some further tests."

'Course they would with an MRI kicking off at a thousand euros a pop. I said,

"Don't hold your breath."

He gasped,

"I beg your pardon?"

In that prissy tone that warrants a serious puck in the mouth. Outside, I deep breathed and looked at my hand, shaking like the last gasp of a wino.

A distinguished-looking guy in a dressing gown was looking lost and trailing an IV. Hard to look impressive in that gear but he managed. He asked,

"Is there an area for smoking?"

Not anymore.

I said,

"Not anymore."

He said,

"Life is full of irony. I had not smoked for years then, with this health scare, I started again and now there is nowhere you *can* actually practice the foul deed."

I said,

"Go ahead, I'll deal with the fallout."

He looked at me anew, said,

"That is awfully generous of you. This world needs more of your thinking."

I seriously doubted that.

He lit up, dragged deep like only a former smoker can, guilt and relief dancing that waltz of addiction. He gasped,

"My word, that is good."

Then reveled in the hit, said,

"Inherent vice."

Quick as a first-year lit wanker, I said,

"Thomas Pynchon."

He was impressed, said,

"Erudite too."

I gave an enigmatic smile as if I knew what that even meant. Then a shout and a galloping security guard appeared, all puff and indignation, shouted,

"Hoi, smoking is forbidden."

He looked at me. I said,

"Verboten."

He went,

"What?"

"German,"

I said.

He looked at the smoker, snarled.

"I don't give a toss where you're from but no smoking here."

I got right in his face, hissed,

"I know you and wonder does your employer know you used to have a thing for wee kiddies?"

He stepped back, said,

"That was never proven."

I smiled.

He weighed his options, then,

"I'll let it slide this time but don't let me catch you here again."

I had full respect for the man who continued to smoke, watching the exchange with almost disinterest. I said to the security guy,

"Run along now. Must be a car or two needs clamping."

He sized me up, said,

"I'll remember you."

And slunk off.

The man dropped his cig, said,

"You have a way with you."

I held out my hand, said,

"Jack Taylor."

He shook it warmly, said,

"Jeremy Cooper."

The Late Sixties in every sense of the word seemed to be dying.

Glenn Frey (67)

Lemmy (70)

David Bowie (69)

Alan Rickman (69)

It was either a very dangerous age or

Extremely fortunate to have reached that decade.

Trump was leading the polls in the U.S. and it seemed as if he were giving vent to all the voiceless and then he got the endorsement of Sarah Palin.

Phew.

To see them embrace in Iowa was to see ignorance and prejudice entwined. Their smiles of glee sent a shiver along every line of reason you ever had. The water cooler moment in Ireland was the screening of the documentary series *Making a Murderer.*

With

The Jinx.

Podcast of *Serial.*

The public was transfixed with true crime. Then, to add ridicule to disbelief, Sean Penn literally led the authorities to capture *Chappie.*

He wrote an article in *Rolling Stoma* that was a crash course in a little knowledge being so dangerous.

No wonder I drank.

Ghost No. 1, Jeremy Cooper, was back from his unexpected trip to the hospital. He had been stunned when the doctors told him his prognosis was bad, well . . . dire.

People react to such news in so many different ways.

Anger

Disbelief

Fear

All of the above.

Cooper wanted a cigarette.

His whole dream of ruling the city with his army of ghosts was just smoke in the Galway wind. Woody, his second in command, could see something was seriously wrong. His boss, his messiah, was weakened and, Christ, he looked sick. Cooper said,

"Our grand schemes are fucked."

Obscenities from the master!

Cooper sighed, then,

"Get me a cigarette."

That in itself was the sign of how things were. Previously, cigarettes were part of the list Cooper had banned. Not that Woody had stopped smoking; he'd stopped only in front of the boss. So he had to make a show of going to fetch some. He asked his own self,

"Fuck, now what?"

The ghosts were going to be famous and powerful and . . .

He tore open a pack of cigarettes, lit one, fumed in every sense.

He had managed to recruit ten followers, and what would he tell them now?

"Sorry guys, Armageddon is deferred."

Traipsed back to Cooper, depression laying heavy on his mind. Cooper took a cig, fired up, then,

"Change of plan, if we're going out, let us go out in style."

Woody had no idea what this meant so said nothing. Cooper chucked the cig, said,

"Something major, have them gasp and exclaim, *There be ghosts.*"

Then Copper paused, thought. Said,

"At the hospital, I met a man who might be suitable for our plans. His name is Jack Taylor and, if I had to hazard a guess, I'd say you would find him in a pub."

Woody felt a tinge of resentment, as if he was being considered less vital. Cooper caught the

Sense, soothed,

"I am blessed with you my man."

Neither of them felt it carried much conviction.

Woody was in a quandary. He had so fervently believed the ghosts were the answer to everything but now Cooper was sounding very much like a guy who was quitting. Rage was simmering in every pore. He needed some fix to put him back on some meaningful track.

Confession.

His mother had gone faithfully every Saturday to be absolved for her sins. It didn't seem to make her life a whole lot better but for a brief time she would be light and even singing. Fuck, he thought, a brief respite would be just fine.

Rang around the churches to see what times confessions were being held. Riled to find a tone of suspicion not to mention downright hostility from most of the churches. First lesson, it was no longer called confession but, get this,

"The sacrament of reconciliation."

"But,"

He pleaded,

"Is it the same gig?"

Meaning,

"Will I be forgiven?"

The voice on the other end was beyond supercilious, sneered,

"I am hardly in a position to judge that."

The sarcasm was loud and meant. Woody was enraged, said,

"Before I get forgiven, I'll add you to my list of wrongdoing."

Slammed down the phone. Eventually got times for the Cathedral. Headed up there.

Nervous now so stopped at the pub off Mary Street. A place where if you knew even one name of the Kardashians you were barred. Sunk two large Jamesons and, thus fortified, headed for reconciliation.

At the church, business was brisk. Post-Christmas blues providing a steady stream of folk keen to get something free, like forgiveness. Saw a young priest head into the confessional and thought,

Young is more likely to be accessible. The old codgers were holy terrors.

Got in there and began,

"Forgive me Father."

Which was a bad start as he was at least twenty years older than the priest.

Then the booze hit and he amended.

"Whoa, hold the bloody phones, I forgive God."

The young priest had been schooled in most situations but not this, he tried,

"I beg your pardon?"

Woody was having none of it, the Jameson flowing mad through his system. He echoed and mimicked.

"You beg my pardon? Too bloody right, mate, and you know what, I ain't giving it."

And then stormed out of the confessional, banged the door in as far as is possible in a church, ranted at the assembled penitents,

"Get up off your knees, have some fucking backbone."

He was gone by the time the Guards arrived.

"Now that he was no longer subject to institutional rules governing brutality he felt free to hit people at will."

(Kate Atkinson, *Started Early, Took My Dog*)

Back she came.

Emily.

Waiting in my apartment when I returned from walking the pup. The pup went apeshit with delight on seeing her so, no matter how I felt about her, it would always be tempered by the affection he felt for her. She was dressed like Jennifer Lawrence in *American Hustle*, all bad-ass grunge. I said,

"Nice to see you have no compunction about breaking into my place."

Was she fazed?

Was she fuck.

Said,

"Mi cassia es su cassia"

She delighted in mangling language, any language. Then,

"Your neighbor is climbing Everest?"

She and Doc had had a brief, insane fling, which was a touchy subject for all of us. I asked,

"You guys are talking again?"

"Fuck no, I broke into his place."

The last thing you ever did was ask her why, ever. She said,

"He might have to change them plans of glory."

Now I had to ask,

"Why?"

She gave that smile of utter mischief, said,

"His tickets, itinerary?"

Made a whoosh with her hands, said in child's voice,

"All gone."

I shook my head, said,

"But you have to know he will have everything backed up on his laptop?"

The smile widened.

"No laptop, not no more, *things we lost in the fire.*"

"You set a fire?"

Wonderment now on her face, she said,

"No, you think I should?"

Man, she would exhaust a pope, and an infallible one at that. She said,

"The ghosts of Galway?"

"What?"

"Would be political shakers, tossers and losers really, I fucked one of 'em."

"Where the hell is this going?"

Ignoring my question, she continued,

"That red book they think is some sort of magical oracle, I borrowed it from them."

I said,

"I have not been so completely lost since the last episode of *The Sopranos.*"

She sighed dramatically, asked,

"You want the short version?"

"Please."

The pup had given up and was snoring not so quietly in her lap. She said,

"*The Red Book* is supposed to be some sort of ecclesial time bomb. It isn't, just a rip-off version of *The Book of Kells*. So a rogue cleric steals it, gets snuffed by the ghosts, and I relieve those idiots of it but they now have a new plan."

I said,

"Let's pretend I follow this. What is the ghost plan?"

She gave me the look that says

"For fuck's sake."

Then very patiently,

"They tried to get the attention of people by dumping animals in the square. Not a whole amount of interest so now they have devised a grand scheme."

She rooted in her Marc Jacobs bag. I knew the bag as it said in bold letters *Marc Jacobs*. Produced a pack of Gauloises (they still made those?), then a chunky Zippo and fired up. In seconds we were on a Parisian boulevard and I asked,

"Thought you were into that whole new e-cig, vaping gig?"

Shook her head amid the cloud of French nicotine, said,

"That's when I was a poseur."

"And now?"

"I'm just a gal who got real."

If ghosts there be
The ghosts of Galway
Are the whisper
You thought you heard
Along the wind that howls
From across the bay,
The wind that screams in the seconds
Before you wake
Touching you below
The shred of belief
You thought you had.

I was in the GBC, the old-style café off Eyre Square. Old-style in that they still treat you like you might matter. Frank Casserly is chef there for going on twenty years. If it is true that

Men cook to show off

And

Women cook so that people can eat

Then Frank is the exception to that. He cooks because it is his job. I had once rather foolishly asked him,

"Is it your vocation?"

Got the look and

"Don't be a stupid bollix, Jack."

Meaning I might be able to alter the *stupidity* but not the other.

I had just finished the neon nightmare of

Two fried eggs

Black pudding

Three rashers

Two fat sausages

Fried mushrooms

Thick white toast.

The carbs mutiny.

And supposedly the only real cure for a hangover. The thinking being that, if you can face that, how much were you hurting to begin with?

I came out and an outlaw shard of sunshine led me to beach on the square. Was lighting a cig, feeling if not optimistic, at least not suicidal. A young girl, fourteen at most, approached. She had that urchin look, like an escapee from a Dickens movie. The Orphan Annie vibe. Maybe Emily could adopt that for her next guise?

She marched right up to me, stated,

"Mr. Taylor."

God only knew what she would want, so I snapped,

"Whatever it is you want or are proposing the answer is *no*."

I felt almost righteous in my determination. She rocked back on her heels, said,

"How terribly rude."

I waved her away, said,

"Whatever."

She got right in my face, smelt vaguely of baby powder and good toothpaste, said,

"My teachers say I am advanced beyond my years and you, *you*, will do me the courtesy of hearing me out."

I sighed, asked,

"And will you fuck the way off then?"

Stuck a finger in my face, said,

"Do not use that foul language to a young girl."

Short of walloping her, she wasn't going away. I said with deep resignation,

"Let's hear your sad story."

Now, hands on hips, she declared,

"Sarcasm does not become you, Mr. Taylor. I had heard you retain a shred of decency."

She'd heard wrong but I gave her my look of rapt attention. She took a deep breath, said,

"My little brother, Eamon, he is twelve, ran away from home, and I want you to bring him back."

I shook my head, said,

"Go to the Guards."

She gave me a look of scrutiny that only utter innocence can bestow and she saw nothing that promised the world would cut her any slack. She produced a battered purse, I think it might have had Our Lady of Perpetual Help on it, rooted in it, and came up with a handful of notes, said,

"I've been saving up for a bike but here, you take it."

There are very few times I have much regard for my own self but right there I was verging on complete disgust. I asked,

"How much is there?"

She rolled her eyes, said,

"Hello, maybe nineteen euros."

My cup finally overfloweth.

She added,

"I will need a receipt for that."

Of course.

I asked,

"And your name?"

"Lorna."
I muttered,
"Lorna Doone."
Exasperated, she snapped,
"No, silly. Dunphy."
I asked,
"Have you a photo?"
She produced a thick envelope, said,
"Everything is in there.
School
Age
Description
And my contact details."
Paused
As if she heard something.
Then,
"I have to run."
And run she did.
When I got back to the apartment I opened the package.
It was reams of blank paper.
I got on Google search and did indeed find her.
She was an only child.

I was walking the pup up the town and he didn't much take to the mime artists. They spooked him.

Me too.

Heard,

"By the holy, Taylor."

Father Malachy. My nemesis. The bane of my life in so many ways. We had a varied history and most of it bad. He stopped, cloud of nicotine over him, stared at the dog. Asked,

"Did you steal that poor creature?"

Low growl from the pup. He could sense my feelings instinctively. Not that he saw Malachy as a threat but rather a nuisance, like a bedraggled cat. Not to chase but to chastise.

Worked for me.

I said,

"Still smoking, eh?"

Ignored that, said,

"I've been thinking of your poor mother."

Fuck, here we go.

I said,

"We all have our crosses."

Looked like he wanted to wallop me, said,

"I think the poor woman was bipolar."

Oh, man, I fucking laughed out loud, mimicked,

"Bipolar! Fucking beautiful, the greatest bitch to walk the earth and now it's, like, *oh, she couldn't help it.*"

He gave me a look bordering almost on pity, said,

"You are a bitter man."

Just then, the girl Lorna Dunphy passed by, stopped, asked, no, demanded,

"Did you find my brother?"

Before I could answer, Malachy said,

"Lorna, run along now."

And she did!

I stared at him and he rounded on me, near spat,

"Hope you haven't been putting notions in that girl's head?"

Jesus wept.

I said,

"She hired me to find her nonexistent brother."

His eyes were on fire from rage and he accused,

"You took money from that poor creature?"

"Yeah, all of nineteen euros."

He blessed himself, said,

"There is no end to your wickedness. That child suffers."

I was all out of patience with the craziness that seemed to have infected the whole city, snarled,

"Let me guess, bipolar?"

He dismissed that with a wave of his hand, said,

"You are a heartless excuse for a man."

I ignored that, persisted.

"What is it with that girl, eh?"

He sighed, said,

"Like everyone else who has had dealings with you, she simply wanted one simple thing."

I had to ask.

"What might that be?"

Like I could give a full fuck.

He said,

"To get your attention."

Back at the apartment, I drew up a list of all the bizarre threads of my current life.

Who, what, were the ghosts of Galway?

What was the deal with the girl and the imaginary brother?

The Red Book.

Emily . . . Always Emily and her diffuse weirdness.

My former boss.

The dead ex-priest.

Sat back, looked at it.

Made no sense.

Tried to think how a thriller writer would throw out all these strands and then, presto, wrap them all up with a rugged hero, battered but unbowed, heading into an award-winning future.

I looked at the pup, asked,

"Got any ideas?"

He stared at the leash.

A pounding at the door put the heart sideways in me. The pup went into attack mode. I pulled the door open to a young Guard. I mean so young he seemed like a child in dress-up but what was old was his attitude. Already bitter and malignant, he near shouted,

"Are you . . ."

Consulted his notes.

"John Trainor?"

"No."

Rattled him.

If it was in the notebook, it had to be true. He tried,

"Name?"

I said,

"Jack Taylor."

Again with the notebook, then,

"Your neighbor was burgled, you know anything about that?"

"No."

"Mind if I have a look inside?"

"Got a warrant?"

He had obviously watched lots of cop shows, asked in a tough tone,

"Wanna play hardball?"

"I want to know if you have a warrant. If not, fuck off."

Kinda hardball.

He reeled back, lost for a moment. I said,

"Get Sergeant Ridge."

"She know you?"

"She'd know where to look."

And I shut the door. Heard him mutter about dog license. The pup didn't seem too concerned.

* * *

Over the years, I've made one hell of a lot of bad decisions. If there was a bad way to do things, I was your guy. Whatever about *the road less traveled,* I always took the road to despair. Be nice to think I'd learned from experience.

Nope.

Now, as I surveyed the list of bafflements, I thought I really needed to know what the deal was with the girl who claimed to have a missing brother.

Lorna Dunphy.

Found where she lived easily. Or where her home was. Off Merchants Road. A small beleaguered section of old Galway that still hadn't fallen to the developers. Put on my Garda all-weather, black 501s, my Doc Martens with the steel toe caps, and figured I was ready for just about anything.

Figured wrong.

Met my neighbor Doc outside my door, asked,

"You think I stole your laptop?"

Gave me a look of utter derision, said,

"Who else?"

I'd been obviously watching too much *Sherlock* as I said,

"Succinct."

Well, beats the ubiquitous *whatever.*

Halve the distance between A and B
Halve it again
Then again
Until infinity.
You will never reach B.

(Zeno)

I stood for a moment outside Lorna Dunphy's home, took a deep breath. Then knocked and waited. Door opened and a man appeared, maybe in his battered forties. Something had beaten the hell out of him and, when he was on his knees, life had kicked him in the balls. He was wearing old cord Levi's, a faded sweatshirt with the logo for the Saw Doctors, though it was a long time since this man heard any music. Does anyone remember desert boots? This man did and was wearing them. He had a tangle of dark curly hair, long from not caring and not fashion. He asked,

"Is this about Lorna?"

A soft voice, laden with foreboding, he knew most calls were *about Lorna.*

I nodded, said,

"I'm truly sorry to bother you."

For once I truly meant it.

He waved me in, not even asking who I was. Led into a sitting room that was so tidy it seemed unlived in. A single framed photo of a woman, with her head back, laughing. He motioned me to a chair, asked,

"Would you like a drink?"

Not *tea or coffee*?

I know the inflection so well, my whole life constructed around it.

I said,

"That would be good."

Even fucking vital.

He got a bottle of Redbreast; they even make that anymore? Two heavy Galway crystal tumblers, poured nigh lethal measures, handed me one. The glass felt almost reassuring. I didn't think a toast was in order. He sat opposite, his glass placed carefully on a small table beside him.

I said,

"I'm Jack Taylor."

Then, oh fuck, he got up, held out his hand, said,

"Tom."

I took a mega hit of the drink and it walloped my stomach, both bitter and comforting. I said,

"Your daughter, um . . ."

He sighed, with a resignation that no one should have, asked,

"What she do now?"

I wanted a cig, took out the pack, offered one.

He took it, leaned over, picked up one of those family-size boxes of matches, and lit it, the sound like a pistol shot. I lit my own quietly. We fumed for a bit then I said,

"It's just she is telling people she has a brother and he is missing."

He groaned.

I tried,

"I'm sure it's just a phase."

Lame, huh?

He pointed at the framed photo, said,

"Her mother, Ann."

Nothing more.

But his face was ruin, sadness and despair battling for supremacy.

Then he asked,

"You know Barna Woods?"

I knew of it.

I just nodded.

He said,

"There's a tree there that they supposedly favor."

I didn't have to ask

Who *they* were.

Suicides.

He continued, a story he had to recount over and over and never understand.

"Used a rope I had for a camping trip we had planned."

Stopped, asked,

"You like camping?"

WTF?

I tried,

"Not really."

He sighed, said,

"Me neither, but Ann . . ."

Gulped.

"Ann said it would be fun to do as a family."

Aw, fuck, fuck, fuck.

I said,

"I'm very sorry."

He stood up, said,

"Please excuse me. I have to do some serious drinking."

At the door, he asked,

"What will become of Lorna?"

I lied fast.

"She will be fine."

We both smiled at that piss weak lie.

God knows, whatever else would happen to the girl, fine wouldn't be part of it.

I thought about mothers.

Freud said that if a child was deeply encouraged, loved, praised, the adult would always be chock-a-block with confidence and self-belief.

Okay, Freud probably didn't actually say *chock-a-block*. I mean, who the fuck does apart from debutantes, but you get the drift.

My mother was the bitch from many versions of hell. Her gig was to sneer, ridicule, and belittle.

Signs on.

I mean,

Look at me!

Was there a tree in Barna that lured suicides? Kind of a chilling thought and why the fuck didn't someone chop that fucker down? On a completely different horror note, the elections were announced. The government was finally going to hear how the people felt about the water levies and all the other issues like housing and health they had so blithely dismissed addressing. Of course, we had the sneering jackal face of the leader threatening he would be back and, get this, in his own constituency of Mayo, he called people who dared to question

"Whimpers."

And worse? In Irish terms anyway,

"Whiners!"

I walked to Shop Street and a busker/mime was massacring "Delilah."

Yeah, the awful song by Tom Jones, the guy was wailing,

"Why,

Why,

Why?"

I implored,

"Jeez, give it a bloody rest."

He did stop, then,

"You can't handle real talent."

I had no answer for that so I put twenty euros in his box. He looked at it, said,

"You call that fair wage?"

You can't really take back the money but by Christ I was tempted. I got a newspaper. It was all election fever. Polls predicted annihilation for the Labour party. Their leader Joan

Burton was detested on a national level not seen since Henry's hand ball knocked us out of the World Cup. Families who had been Labour folk for generations were simply disgusted. Rarely had a politician so misjudged the mood of the people.

Trump continued his blitzkrieg of hate and bullying. And he continued to lead.

Sean O'Casey wrote

"The world is in a state o' chassis."

Was that ever the truth.

On a wall I saw,

"The ghosts are coming."

I didn't think it was a rock group.

On hookers: *It's not the work,*
It's the stairs.

There is a line from *Carousel*, the gist of which is,

As

Long

As

One

Person

Remembers

You

It

Isn't

Over.

Now you might wonder about the state of mind of someone who knows the lyrics to that musical but Jeremy Cooper, the proclaimed *ghost* of Galway, had a mind clutter fucked with trivia.

Dressed now in a black Hugo Boss leather jacket, black combat jacket, Doc Martens, he was about one hour away from a murder occurring. He reminded his own self of an Irish version of Mosley but, hey, he muttered,

"Who even knew of Mosley anymore?"

Or,

Utilizing his Trinity education, Mosley's connection to the Mitford sisters? He'd said that to Woody, his second in command, and Woody asked,

"They like, um, the Spice Girls?"

Help was indeed hard to get, but to ask for intelligent help?

Yeah, right.

He considered the doctor's verdict, perhaps only months to live.

Fuck.

Still, the painkillers were mega and enveloped him a warm fuzzy cloud. The doctor intoning,

"Use them sparingly as they are very potent."

Oh, yeah, sure thing.

He'd gone back to smoking. Why the fuck not?

Thought back to the past year, phew-oh. Had started with a jewel.

Emerald.

The treacherous Emily. So, okay, he had wondered why a young and, yes,

Hot

Babe would be interested in him.

She wasn't.

She loved to mind fuck and by God she'd sure fucked his. He had told her of his dream to lead a new religion, Ghosts, of the Irish fundamental past. Like she gave a toss. Told her of the elusive *Red Book* and how a rogue cleric, hiding in Galway, had it in his possession.

She said,

"Dan Brown lite."

That should have warned him.

It didn't.

When you think with your dick, you get shafted. Then Woody, the mad bollix, not only found the book but stuffed pages of it in the mouth of the rogue priest.

Zealous?

You betcha.

She then stole it from him.

Unleashed Woody on her who had a local crew beat her half to death.

What a freaking mess.

Deep in his heart, Cooper knew *The Red Book* was shite. A book that had gained a rep purely because no one had actually read it (see current bestseller literary lists).

Truth to tell, though, it was Emerald who had listened to him rant.

"I want to start a movement that will have people talking about it."

She had stared at him with those odd eyes; times you'd swear they were truly green. Then she asked,

"And then, what will you do when you have a following."

He told the truth.

"Abuse them."

She laughed.

"Truly a church, then."

Then added,

"First you have to get their attention."

True.

So he asked,

"And the best way to do that is?"

"Dump dead animals in Eyre Square."

"Why?"

She sighed,

"If you want to be noticed these days, you have to be outrageous."

He nodded.

Made sense.

She had introduced him to the Chinese game of Go. Said,

"Needs more skill than chess."

He focused all his attention when they played, while she affected to be bored shitless.

Said,

"I'm bored shitless."

And beat him every time. He once found her playing her own self. She said,

"I have enough personalities to play five times myself."

Whatever that meant.

Nothing good.

She loathed Woody, told him,

"You make Trump seem intelligent."

Woody was in awe of her, said,

"Pity the cunt is so gorgeous."

Words to live by.

The temptation to have Woody finish the job and kill Emerald had its attraction.

Pure and ice cold payback.

But

A world without her in it?

No.

She made him feel that anything was possible. Even the mad notion of starting a Galway clone of Scientology. Was Ghosts even a creditable name?

He looked at his watch. It was just slightly over half an hour until he was a witness to murder.

Emily had watched

Lady Vengeance,

And so this morning she laid out a personality starting with

Envy,

Building through

Resentment

To outright fury.

Picked up her phone, called the Garda station,

Asked,

In a Scottish accent,

"May I speak to Sergeant Ridge?"

No,

They said.

So she screamed,

"There is going to be a killing."

Got Ridge who spat,

"What is this?"

Emily felt a warm glow, said,

"My dad, Jeremy Cooper, lives in the Mews, Taylor's Hill, a man named Woody is holding him hostage."

Then she screamed, primarily to put the heart sideways in Ridge.

It worked.

Not that it is easy to scream in a Scottish accent. Then to gild the rose, she said, almost offstage as it were,

"Oh, mi Gad, the wee man has a gun."

Then crashed the phone down on the table, near deafening Ridge.

In suitable dramatic fashion the phone went dead or, as they might remark in Glasgow,

"Deed"

Ridge had been having a real bad day. Superintendent Clancy had given her a bollixing about not solving the animals' dump and roared,

"The fuck is this I hear about Ghosts of Galway?"

She wanted to say,

"Bullshit, urban paranoia."

But when you are

1. A female Guard
2. Gay

You, as they say in Jane Austen speak,

Demur.

Least she thought they said that but it translated as

"Shut your fucking mouth."

She did.

Then,

"Sir, there is a report of a shooting in Taylor's Hill."

He misheard or maybe it was wishful thinking, barked,

"Someone shot Taylor? Thank Christ."

She delicately rephrased.

He was not pleased, shouted,

"Why are you still here then?"

Emily then called Jeremy and, as fate would have it, Woody answered. She said,

"Compadre, we have had our differences but we are allies in our respect for Jeremy."

Pause.

Woody wondered what a *compadre* was.

She continued, silk voice that never failed to entice.

"There is a woman coming right now to hurt *our* Jeremy and the sly bitch is posing as a Guard."

He near shouted,

"Won't fool me."

Emily had to bite down, then,

"Of course not, that's why you are Jeremy's most trusted confidant."

Had she overdone it?

Heard a racking sound, Woody asked,

"Hear that?"

"Yes?"

"That is the nine millimeter being racked."

Emerald had one brief moment of doubt, then, *fuck it,*

Said,

"Be careful . . . Woody."

He gulped, then,

"Bring it on Guard bitch."

Ridge had difficulty finding backup as most of the force was on duty at yet another water protest. No matter how the public howled, the government sneered.

"You will pay those charges."

The people said,

"Screw you,"

And, hallelujah, voted them out of power.

Suck that.

She finally secured a young Guard named Murphy and, no, not nicknamed Spud. You have to have a modicum of interest to invest in a nickname and, in Murphy, there was none.

Why?

He didn't play hurling.

Sacrilege.

He couldn't care less. Like all the youth, as soon as he got a visa, he was off to Australia. He was what used to be called a *callow* youth.

It fit.

All the squad cars were at the water protest so Ridge took a battered Corolla, used by the Drug Squad. Murphy asked,

"Will I drive?"

Ridge said,

"Shut the fuck up unless you are spoken to."

Murphy could already envision his future in Australia: barbecues and Foster's.

Outside Jeremy Cooper's home were a riot of bushes, small trees. Once lovingly cared for by the Poles but they had long since fucked on home, the Celtic Tiger but a dead memory.

Woody lay in wait behind a juniper, the nine in his hand like a discarded prayer, there but not yet utilized.

Madness ran wild through his head.

Muttering,

Bloody priest treating me like shite,

Cops always on my case.

Women laughing at him.

At him.

By Jesus.

Ridge parked the car and they got out. Woody watched them, thought,

Can't be cops driving a Corolla.

They moved to the door and Ridge banged hard on it. Woody stepped out from the bushes, said,

"Don't knock like that, have some fucking manners."

Ridge looked at him, saw a scrawny youth with a stupid expression, and spat,

"Get over here."

To him.

Orders.

From a damn woman.

He didn't move and Murphy, gung ho, added,

"Get your arse in gear and I mean *now.*"

Now?

Woody raised the nine and for one frozen moment it could have been averted if Ridge hadn't moved toward him.

He shot her in the face.

Murphy, in disbelief, muttered,

"What?"

Woody shot him twice in the stomach.

Woody stood over them and fired one more shot in Murphy's head, said,

"Ghosts two,

Assholes nil."

PART 2

A bespoke girl
Tailormade, as it were,
Would require one vital quality.
(A sense of humor,
Because she was going to fucking need it.)

I was in Crowe's pub in Bohermore when a guy burst in, said,

"Two Guards have been shot."

Mad conversations erupted and Ollie shouted,

"Quiet, I'll turn on the radio."

Utter silence as we heard that two Garda had been killed, a massive manhunt was under way. The killer, or killers, were not yet identified and no one had claimed responsibility. The names of the fallen Guards were being withheld until relatives were informed.

All eyes turned to me.

Once a Guard, always a Guard.

Even a disgraced one like me might have some *in*.

I took out my phone, said,

"I'll see what I can do."

Scattered shouts of

"Good man."

There is a kind of horrified delight in unveiling tragedy and a dark thrill at bearing witness.

I called Owen Daglish, just about the only contact I had remaining in the Guards.

Ridge had been my go-to gal for so long but she wasn't answering my calls these days.

Owen began,

"Jesus Jack, you can't be calling me."

He was a piss artist of epic scale and still managed to stay on the force. He kept his head down and was a hell of a manager of the hurling squad. To manage hurlers, you needed to be ferocious and drink didn't hurt in adding the layer of aggression.

He took a deep breath, said,

"Seriously Jack, this is not a good time, all hell is breaking loose."

Time to fake him out.

I said,

"Me heart is broken with the shootings."

He was taken aback, asked,

"You know, then?"

I gave a bitter laugh, said,

"Superintendent Clancy and I may seem at odds"—to put it fucking mildly—"but we go back a ways."

He bought it, said,

"I know you were once close to Sergeant Ridge and I am truly sorry for your loss."

WTF?

I remember mimicking,

"Sergeant Ridge?"

He said,

"Yes, died at the scene, and the young recruit Murphy died en route to hospital."

* * *

The double funeral was held on a bitter cold Thursday. Crowds lined the street.

I have only vague recollections of the whole awful event. Trying to offer my condolences to Superintendent Clancy, who snapped,

"You don't belong here."

I indicated Ridge's coffin, asked,

"Does she?"

Yeah, I know.

Beyond lame.

At the graveside, Father Malachy intoned,

"Man is full of misery."

And I shouted,

"Aw, don't say that."

I got into a minor scuffle with the priest and, phew-oh, they threw me out of the cemetery.

Got to be a first, barred from the graveyard.

Guess it would be cremation then.

My mobile shrilled and in my utter madness I half thought it might be Ridge. It was Emily, who went,

"Wassup?"

Jesus.

I said,

"I'm kind of fucked here, Em."

"Where are you?"

"At Rahoon Cemetery."

She laughed, said,

"Don't let 'em bury you."

I met her in what used to be the River Inn. That there is not a river within a spit of that pub is neither here nor there. Like so many other pubs, it was now under new management and called

The Sliding Rock.

No, me neither.

There is a sliding rock in Shantalla. A Galway landmark to generations of children but now more in use with the ubiquitous drinking schools.

I was working on a full pint when Emily showed.

Who was she today?

Dressed in black leather, her hair in black synch, I asked,

"A Johnny Cash vibe?"

Got the look and,

"Seriously?"

I said,

"I give up. It's not like I could really give a fuck."

She sat, signaled to the guy behind the counter, said,

"Christie Hyde."

The barman came over and oddly enough? Was actually Irish. He was not accustomed to being summoned. He snapped,

"Yeah?"

Like I said, Irish.

Despite what the Brits had believed, we were not born to serve. Emily didn't look at him, said,

"Margarita."

He nearly smiled at me. Translation:

"You poor bastard."

He said to her,

"Think you're in the wrong establishment."

Waited a long beat.

Then added,

"*Love.*"

Fuck me but women hate that sneered endearment.

She turned the full wattage of those sometimes green through blue eyes, asked,

"You got tequila?"

He was into it, running the bitch, he thought. Said,

"Hello? 'Course we got it."

She said in a very Texan accent,

"Then y'all put that in a tall glass and my dad here will add the bitterness."

Phew.

He nodded, turned to go, and she said,

"Yo, Paddy, don't ever call me *love.*"

He headed back to the bar, trying to walk like he hadn't had his arse handed to him.

When the drinks came, she toasted me with

"Good result, eh?"

What?

I stared at her, hoping I wasn't horrendously correct in what was uncoiling in my fevered mind. I asked softly,

"What do you mean?"

Seemed two bullied lifetimes before she answered.

"The bitch is dead."

I had my drink mid-lift, stopped.

Asked in real low tone, menace dripping from every slow enunciation.

"Who is *the bitch*?"

She usually was so on the ball, saw peril before it even finished its coil, but was now on a tequila dance that was blind to nuance, said in jolly voice,

"*Sergeant* smartass Ridge, fixed her good. She bought the farm and all its equipment."

I snatched her wrist, as rough as I could, snarled,

"You reckless cunt, what did you do?"

First time in all our multifaceted dealings that I ever saw fear in her eyes. She near whispered,

"I just made a call, told her of a situation that required Garda help."

Pause.

"I also called Woody, hinted the cops might be en route."

I took a deep drawn-out breath, asked,

"Who the fuck is Woody?"

She was regaining some control, the usual cockiness reasserting itself, said,

"Christ, you never listen, I have told you, the Ghosts of Galway?"

I sat back, trying to absorb the sheer insanity of it all, managed one question.

"This *Woody*, he a shooter?"

Smile on her face, said,

"He is now."

I had so many avenues to respond to this revelation and all,

All,

Of them

Involved violence.

She took my silence as some twisted form of, if not approval, then assent. She said,

"I will admit she was hot in the bed."

Holy fuck!

How is it possible to be simultaneously shocked, stunned, outraged, and absolutely homicidal? Too, I have rarely been lost for words. I have done silence but only because I was too pissed to talk, but a situation where I actually couldn't find a response in my muddled mind? I stared at her and she gave me that radiant smile, said,

"Keep your enemies close, right Jack-o?"

Did I lean over the table and punch her in the mouth?

I stood up, said quietly,

"Get a lawyer."
Confused her. She asked,
"You going to shop me, lover?"
I said,
"To draw up your last will and testament."

"It is possible to
Dig up past misdeeds
So they become
A blight,
A veritable plague."

(Alcoholics Anonymous)

Nun, *but the brave and the rash.*

I went to see a nun, weird as that is.

Me!

With a nun as a friend.

Years ago, I had helped out the Church and a nun, Sister Maeve, believed I did miraculous work.

I didn't but take it where you can. We developed a curious friendship and she was always available for pup-sitting. Too, the pup loved her. You want to see the measure of a person, see how they behave with a dog. It is as good a litmus test as you could find.

Maeve worked as a conduit between the convent and the public. I really wanted an opportunity to use *conduit* in a sentence and now I was doing it.

I told the pup,

"Let's go see your nun."

Much tail wagging and bouncing off the walls. The death of Ridge, and Emily being the perp, it was more than my mind could bear. A knock at the door. I dunno but for some reason I grabbed my nine millimeter from under the bookcase. I had *acquired* it from a Russian bouncer.

Swear to God, the pup recoiled from that, as if instinctively he knew guns were bad news.

Lock and load.

Opened the door.

A young man who looked vaguely familiar. He said,

"Mr. Taylor, remember me?"

"No."

He was disappointed, said,

"I'm a friend of Em, Emily, Emerald."

The gun was in the waistband of my jeans. I said,

"Don't mean shit to me fellah."

He held out a book

. . . The fucking ubiquitous *Red Book*

He said,

"Emily feels this will make up for the . . ."

Stalled.

Reached

for

the

Least

Offensive

Description.

Got

"Incident."

The gun was up. I shouted right in his face.

"Getting my friend killed is not a *freaking incident.*"

The pup was out, alarmed, and took a lunge at Hayden's pant leg. Hayden yelled,

"Who let the dog out?"

I was of two minds:

Shoot him

Or

Burp him.

I said,

"Come in and watch your tone."

He sat near the bookcase, asked,

"You don't do Kindle?"

Fuck's sake.

I said,

"How do you know the crazy bitch?"

I could not bring myself to utter her name.

He asked, in that new American lilt that young Irish males have adopted,

"Like, you mean Em?"

I said,

"Use that modifier again and I *will* shoot you."

He seemed remarkably unfazed by my threats, asked,

"What's a modifier?"

I sighed, sounding not unlike my dead mother, who could have sighed for Ireland and, in many ways, did.

I said,

"What's the deal with you and . . . *her* . . . are you in a relationship or just her messenger boy?"

Didn't much care for the term, his near constant smile was bruised. He tried,

"She is *like* a sister to me. We go way back."

(Way back these days usually means about a year.)

"And we share, like, a bond. We got each other's back."

Sounding as if he was from lower Manhattan.

He continued.

"I was caught up in the Ghosts of Galway bullshit and Em, she showed me it was just all crap and, like, you know, showed me the light."

"So why are you here again?"

He gave me a smile of such dazzling whiteness that I nearly warmed to him.

Nearly.

The pup seemed to have eased too in his response to him and actually lay at his feet. Hayden said,

"Oh, right."

And then said nothing.

With all the smartphones and technology, young people seemed to lack the ability to pursue a thought. If it wasn't text, it didn't count. I said, with a trace of granite in the words,

"Focus, for fuck's sake."

He looked at me as if seeing me for the first time, asked,

"What's with all the hostility, dude?"

Dude.

I moved right in his face, said,

"Emily? The message. And if you call me *dude* again I'll rearrange your face."

He said,

"Em wants you to know that like, you know, no hard feelings and you can have *The Red Book*. You don't even have to grovel for it."

I stared at him.

I nearly said,

"You're *like* a conduit."

He continued.

"Fat fuck you used to work for?"

I nodded.

"He will pay serious green for it, even though it is, like, bogus."

"Bogus?"

"Yeah, definitively. Em got some scholar to, like, check it out and at best it is *Book of Kells* lite."

Then he reached in his jacket and the pup went on alert. I said,

"Better be a book."

Got the radiant smile and

"You crack me up, *dude*."

Put a very small battered red volume on the table. Stood up, said,

"My work here is done so, like, sayonara."

He stopped at the door, said,

"Em got one thing slightly wrong, though."

"Yeah?"

He looked like he might touch my shoulder but wisely didn't, said,

"You're not seriously old, like she said."

"Jack, you remember how much affection I had for you
Once.
Multiply that by infinity
And that is how much I now
Loathe
You."

(Sergeant Bean NI Iomaire [Ridge]
Last words to Jack.)

"Anybody could be smart. It took a special somebody
To be clever."

(Karin Slaughter, *Pretty Girls*)

Jeremy Cooper had been

Quizzed

Interrogated

Bullied

Screamed at

Pushed

By Clancy and his crew of hard arse detectives.

A Guard gets killed, throw the rule book out the window. Allowed one phone call.

Yeah, right.

Clancy got right in Jeremy's face, asked,

"Why did the call about a shooting name your house?"

Cooper had no idea, said,

"I've no idea."

Clancy head butted him.

The other Guards actually gasped. Jeremy's chair shot backward, spilling him against the wall with a mighty bang. Clancy said,

"Oops."

He looked at the assembled Guards, barked,

"The fuck are you standing 'round for? Find me the bollix who killed Ridge."

Protestants are still fairly thin on the Galway ground. It is believed if you get in legal shit, get a Protestant, a Protestant lawyer. Maybe it's some echo of colonial times or a harking to the whole landowner shite but the best lawyer in town was Robert Preston.

A Prod.

One of the few remaining Ghosts who hadn't dispersed called him and, in jig time, he was at the station.

Trailing Brit fire and legal brimstone.

He stormed up to Clancy, snarled,

"My client looks as if he has been beaten."

Clancy had many previous dealings with Preston, none of them civil. He rasped,

"Suspect fell."

Preston took his client by the arm, said,

"We'll have you out of here in no time."

Cooper was dazed from his fall, said,

"That big bastard attacked me."

Preston smiled. Of such allegations were careers solidified. He said,

"That big bastard is heading for traffic duty."

Clancy strode off, muttering darkly.

As no charges were made, Cooper was free to go, one of the Guards whispering to him,

"We never forgot killers of our own."

Preston was all over him, threatened,

"Would you like to repeat that for my recorder?"

The Guard pushed past Preston, said,

"Check under your car every day, wanker."

Outside, Preston said,

"We need to have those bruises documented."

Jeremy stared at him, as if just registering him, said,

"This is a cluster fuck."

No argument from Preston.

Jeremy continued.

"You know what you need with a cluster fuck?"

He gave a peculiar emphasis to the f-word as if he actually tasted it, said,

"Jack Taylor."

I was still in shock from the loss of Ridge.

That we had never reconciled just added another nasty layer of guilt and remorse to a mind already in grief overload. I was in my armchair, the pup in my lap, doing his tiny best to console me. They know when you are deeply hurt. I was sipping slowly from the newest awful concoction:

Jameson with . . . breath it quiet . . .

Ginger ale.

I know. Heresy.

But I was in that zone where nothing really matters a fuck.

Even besmirching Jameson. The phone rang and the pup's ears lit up. He hoped it might break my funk. And, more importantly, get him a walk. I answered with a weary

"Yeah?"

Like I gave a good fuck.

Heard

"Mr. Taylor? Mr. Jack Taylor?"

"Yeah?"

"This is Robert Preston of Preston Lynch and Associates?"

I said,

"That don't mean shit to me pal."

Nervous laugh, then,

"I have been forewarned you have a somewhat terse form of communication."

"Terse this. Get to the fucking point."

Another chuckle.

I hate fucking chuckles.

He said,

"I can tell you're a card."

What?

I sighed loud and annoyingly.

He said,

"Sorry, defect of my profession, to prevaricate. Thing is, I have a client who may wish to avail your, um . . . *specialized* talent."

Being in the shitty mood I was, I snapped,

"Will cost them."

Intake of breath, then recovery.

"Of course, no one eats for free."

I said,

"Don't be an asshole."

A beat,

Then,

"By Jove, Mr. Taylor, I do believe I like the cut of your jib."

What? Jib?

I said,

"Talk fucking right."

Laughter.

He asked,

"Might we meet in my modest office on Eglantine Street, noon tomorrow?"

I said,

"Like you legal types do, it will cost you for my time, whether I take the case or not."

"I would expect no less. Au revoir."

Did I detect just the tiniest note of sarcasm?

The Red Book?

Meant Jack shit to me. I flipped through it. Whatever it was, it wasn't a patch on *The Book of Kells*. I put it in my bookcase, not entirely sure what I should do with it.

Sell it?

Most likely.

That evening, I was back from the pup's walk. He was knackered. We'd done the walk from the Claddagh along Grattan Road, up to Blackrock, kicked the wall there as is the custom, then back along the beach of Salthill.

What the Brits would call *bracing*.

The pup trotting alongside me, glancing anxiously at me, intuiting that something was badly off. He was right. I walked with a cold fury tightening my heart and strangling my soul.

I would not

Could not

Dwell on Ridge.

I'd settled the pup on his chair, his Galway United scarf wrapped around his neck, poured a large Jay and, with a *phew,* sank into the armchair. A bang on the door.

Not a knock, a full wallop. If this was Jehovah's Witnesses, they'd be witnessing sooner than they anticipated.

Father Malachy.

The pup growled.

Malachy barged in, trailing cigarette smoke, said,

"Need to talk to you?"

I went,

"How'd you know where I lived?"

Gave me a look of

"Seriously?"

Said,

"Google Earth."

The pup glared at him, still low growling. Malachy asked,

"Does he bite?"

"Only priests."

He looked around the room, not seeing anything that made him happy, asked,

"Where am I supposed to sit?"

The thing with Malachy was, you could just wallop him on a full-time basis. I indicated the armchair and he took that, sighing deeply. Then,

"Are you going to wet a man's whistle?"

Even the pup had given up on intimidating him and simply went under the table. I got a glass of Jameson, handed it to him, asked,

"Ice?"

He lit up, coughed, looked like he might throw up, said,

"These boys will be the death of me."

I said,

"We live in hope."

And he looked deeply offended, said,

"No need for that."

I asked,

"The purpose of your visit?"

He lit another cig, no ashtray required. He said,

"I'm in need of a fucking miracle."

This, from a priest.

I asked,

"Have you tried, like, you know, your stock in trade?"

Glared at me, snarled.

"What fierce shite are you suggesting?"

I let that nice turn of phrase hover, then said simply,

"Prayer."

Looked like he might wallop me, said,

"They're downsizing in the Church."

I laughed out loud, said,

"That is such a *holy* terror."

He was serious, said,

"Sending me to some place like *Bally de fucking nowhere*"

I said,

"Like De Niro at the end of *True Confessions*."

Wasted.

He said,

"Unless I could, um . . . pull off something that made them think I was valuable."

Fuck me, was he *playing* me?

I asked,

"Anything in mind to, you know, big you up?"

He looked at me, said nothing.

God, everyone had an angle. I said,

"How did you know I had *The Red Book*?"

He feigned ignorance. What if he was telling the truth, though these days truth and clergy rarely met, but what if? Would one fine unselfish gesture eradicate some of the guilt I felt about the death of Ridge?

* * *

But help this asshole, who'd been the bane of my life? Not to mention my mother's ally.

He was a priest and who in Ireland today would lift a finger for them? Before I could speak, he said,

"People don't like me, it's always been that way. I have no friends."

That kind of fucked with my head. I said,

"My mother?"

He gave a bitter laugh, said,

"She despised me but having a pet priest was a feather in her cap."

I tried,

"Hey, I don't have a whole lot of friends my own self."

Even the dog looked up.

Said,

"Ah, bollocks, when you put your mind to it, people like you well enough. You just don't take any care of their feelings."

Phew-oh.

I gave one last try, said,

"You have your faith to sustain you."

Got the look of utter disdain, he said,

"Yeah, right."

I went to my bookcase, took out *The Red Book*, said,

"This might help put you back in favor."

He took it, put it in his pocket, said,

"I was hoping for money."

A coffin
Makes
It
Difficult
To
Think
Outside
The
Box

I said to the pup,

"I have to go see a lawyer."

He whined. It meant no walk. I continued,

"Has to be done to pay for your treats."

He wasn't convinced, went under the chair and feigned sleep with his back to me. So a good start to the day with the pup pissed off. I wore my all-weather Garda coat, seriously considered arming up. Meeting a lawyer, doesn't hurt to be prepared.

I headed down Shop Street and noticed two Guards, a black band of mourning on their sleeves. Ridge's death hit anew. A busker was murdering "She Moved Through the Fair."

I put some coins in his cap and he scowled at me.

How much better could the day get?

Robert Preston's office was one of those new all-glass affairs. Said two things:

One, we have no secrets here.

Yeah, right.

Two, put a large brick through this.

A very pretty receptionist was not impressed at my appearance, asked,

"Are you delivering something?"

"Bad news?"

Not amused.

I said,

"The name is Taylor and I was *summoned* by the head honcho."

Before she could grill me further, a tall man with one hell of a suit came striding down the corridor, boomed,

"Mr. Taylor."

His hand extended, and I swear gold cuff links with initials.

Like, seriously?

Weren't they outlawed apart from Bond movies?

He said,

"So glad you could make it. Let's step into my office and meet the client."

I recognized the man standing by the window. We'd met outside the hospital. He turned, said,

"Jack, good to see you."

The lawyer offered coffee and then said,

"I will withdraw and let you gents get down to business."

Cooper looked ill, very ill. He said,

"I look fucked, right?"

I went very Irish, said,

"God no, you look mighty."

He sat down and indicated I should do the same, settled himself, said,

"From the time of our encounter, I knew you'd be the man if a chap found himself in a spot of bother."

His tone oozed authority, a man accustomed to minions.

I don't do minion well.

I asked,

"This *spot* of bother. Has it do with the murder of the Guards?"

Granite leaked over my words.

He gave me a searching look, asked,

"You knew them?"

I nodded.

He digested that as he considered his next move, then,

"My second in command, Woody. A good lad if a little impetuous."

I waited, not going to make this easy, he said,

"Perhaps, I stress the *perhaps,* he might have been overzealous in his somewhat misguided loyalty to me."

I said,

"The fuck shot two Guards?"

A fleeting wave of rage in his eyes as the true man peeked out, then it was gone and the sweet affability again, said,

"Good heavens, that would be a leap. My hope is that you, as the resourceful chap you are, might find him before the authorities do."

I said,

"If he killed those Guards, his chances with the authorities would be better than me finding him."

He sat back, a building sneer on his face, said,

"I had you figured as a man with a broader canvas."

I near spat,

"*Broader canvas*? The fuck are you saying?"

He sighed.

"Your rep led one to believe you were something other than the pathetic wretch you now present."

I nearly smiled. It's almost nice to be insulted in literary language; makes a change from the usual *bollix*.

I said,

"I guess you won't be needing my services, then?"

He gave me a look of such disdain that his face tilted. He said,

"You are dismissed, Taylor."

I said,

"Thing is, I will now give all my energy to finding this *Woody*."

Just when I figured I had him pegged, he did an about turn and, in a very pleasant tone, asked,

"Have you ever been to the dogs, Mr. Taylor?"

Was it some kind of metaphor? I went,

"Huh?"

"Not difficult, Mr. Taylor. Like horse racing but with . . ."

Paused.

"*Dogs!*"

He was, I decided, many shades of crazy. I said,

"No."

He reached in his jacket, checked a leather-bound notebook, not unlike police issue, said,

"The second race on the card has a dog named, aptly enough, 'Galway Ghost.'"

"You're telling me this why?"

"Many reasons, mostly nefarious but bottom line, I have a sneaking regard for you."

I said,

"Makes me all warm and valued."

I checked the sports page on my return home. The dog was indeed running and quoted at

14/1.

Phew.

If this were a less bleak narrative, the hero would put the mortgage on the bet, and to the strains of

"Eye of the Tiger."

The dog would at the very last second come from nowhere and win!

Glad rejoicings.

The dog lost.

I didn't back him.

Not one cent.

To mix my metaphors, I not only looked that gift horse in the mouth but let it roar, unbridled. My mobile thrilled after the race and I heard Cooper go

"Oh, dear, so sorry."

I waited.

He continued,

"I truly hope you weren't too burnt with your wager, Mr. Taylor."

I laughed into the phone, startling him. He tried,

"I must say you took the loss well."

I said,

"Didn't back him."

A sharp intake of breath, then,

"Why?"

"Because, as they say in parts of the U.S., you are a lying sack of shit."

I could hear his sharp intake of breath. He said,

"No need for that."

He was offended?

Good.

I said,

"One last thing. You can bet on something."

"Yes?"

"Your mate Woody? Kiss him good-bye."

I clicked off the phone, tired of this bollocks. The pup was at my feet, the leash in his mouth. I asked,

"When did you learn that trick?"

Tail wag.

We went up Prospect Hill, past Crowes pub, then all the way up to the cemetery. Only in Ireland, opposite the graveyard gate, a new shop has opened.

In such a location, you'd think, flowers?

Nope.

Get this:

Bridal

Wear!

I kid thee not.

Was it a subliminal message, get hitched and 'twas then but a hop and a skip to the grave?

Just outside the cemetery gates I replayed a call I had made.

I called my friend Owen Daglish and he confirmed the Guards had nothing to pursue. I asked him about the guy Woody, and he sneered, said,

"An idiot, he couldn't even shoot his mouth off."

"Do you know where he is?"

"Why the fuck would I know that when we're not looking for him?"

"That's a no, then?"

"Good-bye Jack."

Never mind a *person of interest*. He wasn't even a person of indifference.

A guy was standing outside the cemetery gates, greeted,

"Jack, how's it cutting?"

I vaguely recognized him but had no name to go with the recollection so I went the Irish way, said,

"Good to see you."

He indicated the graveyard, said,

"You'd think I was keen to get it over with."

The pup was staring at the graves, his body on alert, as if he knew this was not a place to linger.

The guy shook himself, said,

"Prince was found dead."

I didn't quite know the response to this, so went,

"Really?"

He asked,

"Were you a fan?"

Shite.

I said,

"The guy had some moves."

I began to move off myself and he shouted,

"Did you hear about the priest?"

These days that was a multichoice answer.

A. Molester

B. Married his housekeep (of either sex)

C. Robbed the parish funds

D. All of the above.

I went with the cute answer, which covered my ignorance and hinted I knew other stuff, asked,

"Which one?"

"Father Malachy."

"Oh."

"Yeah, he found some rare old book that the Church was looking for and he's being called to Rome for some mega honor."

Fuck.

I asked,

"How did he find it?"

"Oh, he gave all the credit to Anthony."

"Who?"

"Saint Anthony. The go-to guy for lost things."

I was truly shocked. The treacherous bastard.

The guy said,

"Good for him, eh?"

I now knew what the expression meant.

It stuck in my craw.

Did it fucking ever.

He continued,

"He's going to be on *The Late Late Show.*"

Wonder and enchantment in his tone.

That show was the ultimate Irish accolade. It was said you could do most anything to please your mother (once, by joining the priesthood but now, not so much) but nothing impressed her like being a *Late Late* guest.

He said,

"I heard him on Jimmy Norman's radio show and he was so humble."

I'll bet he fucking was.

I'd heard enough and waved a vague good-bye. He went,

"You know him pretty well."

Phew-oh.

I said,

"Seems like I didn't know him at all."

PURPLE

RAIN

The pup and I got back to the apartment just as the heavens opened. I reached for my keys and the pup began a low growling.

Someone was inside.

I pushed the door slowly open, my keys held forward as a fairly lame weapon. The pup was trembling and it took me a moment to see.

A hundred-pound rottweiler was sitting near the bookcase. I said,

"Fuck."

Then heard,

"Don't be shy, Jack, join us."

Emily

Emerald

Em.

Trouble.

She said,

"Meet Satan."

Of course.

I said,

"I already met the devil."

The pup went under his own chair, peeking warily at Satan. He knew what that dog was:

A killer.

Em pushed a book at me, said,

"In gratitude."

I asked,

"You're thanking me?"

Snap of her head and

"Silly, it's the title, by Jenny Diski, about her relationship with Doris Lessing."

I said,

"That means Jack shit to me."

She loved that, her dog not so much. She said,

"Satan responds to just two commands."

I guessed,

"Kill and kill better."

She laughed.

"How very Sam Beckett."

I should have hated her. She was the reason Ridge was dead but hating her was like blaming the weather; it was just elemental. I asked,

"Aren't you at least a little wary of being here? You had my friend murdered."

She sat forward, the dog gave a low rumble. She said,

"Why I have this lovable beast."

I said,

"Keep him close, you'll need him."

She giggled.

"Threats. I love it. How very alpha of you."

I went to the bedroom, rummaged in the closet, and heard her shout,

"You must be the only person in Ireland going into the closet."

Found the gun, racked the slide, and heard her mutter,

"We know that sound and it tolls for us."

She was right.

I came back, aimed the weapon, said,

"Get that damn monster out of here now or I will shoot him."

Sounding not unlike Liam Neeson in *Taken*.

She scoffed.

"You'd never hurt a dog."

I racked the slide and she was on her feet, going,

"Jesus, all right already. You need to cut back on the caffeine, fellah. I really came to help you."

I kept the gun trained on the dog who watched me with what can only be called malevolent interest. My pup was whimpering quietly beneath the chair. I asked,

"Help?"

"The shooter? Woody? But you need to track him fast. He has a plan."

"What plan?"

She gave a smile of such malign slyness, said,

"To blow the living shit out of Galway Cathedral."

Fuck.
I asked,
"Why?"
She headed for the door, dragging a reluctant Satan, said,
"Because it's there."

"Marilyn's brain was consumed with other thoughts. Of murder. If and when, and where and how, and with what."

(John Sandford, *Extreme Prey*)

Terry Wood was on a high from his murderous acts. Muttered,

"I offed two cops, count 'em, *two*."

He was in a small apartment on Merchants Road. Owned by the Ghosts, it had been purchased in the far too brief days when it seemed like their organization might actually amount to something. Jeremy Cooper had been on a high as money and contributions

Were flowing in.

For a shining moment they believed they could be a contender. Then the gradual dissolution. Cooper had no real policy or plan. He wanted power and, apart from shock value and bullshit, he had nothing.

An Irish Farage, if you will.

Oh, notions.

He had a ton of those.

There was a bookcase along the wall and some bright spark had decided to procure books with *ghost* in the title. Never mind if they had absolutely no relevance to the actual *ghosts* aspiring to be a force.

Like this:

The Long Shadow of Small Ghosts,

Laura Tillman.

A Head Full of Ghosts,

Paul Tremblay.

The Ghost in the Machine,

Arthur Koestler.

Thirteen Ghosts.

The last title hit the meanest shade of irony, in that the actual remaining membership of the Ghosts no longer even amounted to that.

Terry Wood, he said his name aloud,

Then

The abbreviation:

"Woody."

He stared at the gun on the table and knew the smart thing would be to ditch it.

And was he going to do that?

Was he fuck!

He hadn't yet been in touch with the boss, Jeremy Cooper. But he would be pleased?

Wouldn't he?

Mmmm?

He was antsy, adrenaline from the shootings still coursing through him, said aloud,

"Gotta move, gotta boogie."

A knock on the door.

WTF?

Or rather, who the fuck?

Snatched up the gun, pushed it in the back of his jeans, like he'd seen in the movies.

Opened the door, cautiously.

Saw a monster of a dog. And a girl, dressed like some punk wannabe. She did a neat spin, asked,

"Goth or emo?"

He asked,

"Emily?"

Got the wicked smile, and,

"Thelma," and

Indicated the dog.

"Louise."

He spluttered.

"That's not a bitch."

Mean chuckle with

"Boy, you is looking at the bitch."

He wondered how she knew where to find him.

She asked,

"You gonna leave all us young 'uns out here in this cold hall?"

He moved aside.

So fucked in the head was he that he didn't clock her hands. She moved right to the bookcase, the monster dog never taking its dead eyes from Woody. She shrilled,

"Boy, where the drinks be at?"

He didn't know, said,

"I don't know."

She said to Satan,

"Stay."

Began pulling open cupboards, then voiced,

"Voilà."

Pulled a bottle of Jameson from the shelf.

Grabbed two mugs, asked, holding the bottle up,

"Shall I be mammy?"

Sloshed nigh lethal amounts then handed one to Woody, said in her best Scarlett tone,

"We'll always have Tara."

He drank fast, thinking,

"She is nuttier than a whole sack of young rats."

Drowning such rodents had been a childhood passion.

Now she asked,

"Back of your pants fellah, that a weapon or . . . ?"

Let the old hacienda line trail off.

Then reached out a hand, demanded,

"Give it here, young pilgrim."

And he did.

She expertly racked the slide, sang,

Rootin'

Tootin'.

Shot Woody in the side of the head. The shot didn't frighten the dog. In his streamlined world, he did the frightening. Emily looked at the dead man, said,

"Kept the best shot for last."

Then adjusted the surgical gloves and rubbed Satan behind the ears, cooed,

"Who's a good boy?"

“As the sun dips toward the horizon
And darkness gathers around the girls
Neither of them knowing how little time they have left
Before the fire goes out.
Remember how good it felt to burn.”

(Robin Wasserman, *Girls on Fire*)

I was admiring the title for Tom Hanks's new movie.

Not that I have huge respect for TH, seeing him as Jimmy Stewart lite. Or indeed have read much of Dave Eggers, thinking, perhaps wrongly, that he has that whole smug gig going.

I mean really,

A Heartbreaking Work of Staggering Genius.

Come on.

Anyway, back to the title I do like:

A Hologram for the King.

"What do you think of that title?"

He didn't seem to have a whole lot to bark on it either way.

A light knock on the door

And I mean *light.*

As if they didn't want to intrude?

I opened the door and there's a man so good-looking it hurt your eyes. As Woody Allen said,

He took handsome lessons.

Tall of course, not wearing a fedora but had the tone of it. Blond tousled hair, a tan.

Tan!

In Galway.

Age in that bad forty, terrific fifty range. His eyes were a sort of steel gray. He offered a warrant card with a gold badge. *Special branch*?

He asked,

"Mr. Jack Taylor?"

In that tone the schmucks in Vegas used to introduce "*Mr. Frank Sinatra.*"

Yeah, annoying as hell.

His hand was out. I noticed a heavy class ring like they have in the U.S., so American experience?

He said,

"Sheridan. May I come in?"

I asked,

"What, no first name, like Madonna or the late Prince?"

He gave a huge grin and, of course, great teeth, said,

"I heard you were a funny guy."

Nothing in his quiet tone suggested he thought there was anything even remotely humorous. I asked,

"If I say no?"

Bigger grin and

"Then I'd have to shoot you."

Waited a beat.

Then,

"And the cute dog."

I let him in and he strode over to the bookcase, asked,

"You think it's true you can read somebody by what they *read*?"

As I said, his tone, his voice was barely above a whisper but it held a ferocity and steel that was damn impressive.

I said,

"Well, nowadays, skels keep the good stuff on Kindle."

He looked impressed, exclaimed,

"I'm impressed. *Skels!* You obviously have read Andrew Vachss."

The pup gave a soft sigh, not much liking the *shoot the dog* crack, and hid under the sofa. Sheridan indicated a chair, asked,

"May I sit?"

And sat.

Asked,

"Coffee?"

Got to hand it to him, he had some moves, knew how to make an entrance.

I bit down on a slightly dormant aggression, fetched the Jameson, offered.

He laughed, quietly of course, said,

"Tad early but, good Lord, how often does one meet Jack Taylor?"

Bollix.

I poured two bracing measures, said,

"Slainte a match."

He answered,

"Agus leat fein."

I was meant to remark on his command of our native tongue.

I didn't.

Said,

"We have established you know all sorts of shite, but *what*
Exactly
Are you doing here?"

He assumed a grave expression, said,

"There has been a suicide."

I didn't want to know.

I truly did not.

I said,

"Do tell."

Even sounded like I might care.

He said,

"Terence Wood, alleged killer of two Guards, shot his bad self in his very bad head."

Pause.

"Good fucking riddance."

No argument.

I echoed,

"Suicide."

For absolutely no reason, he observed,

"I have lived my life betwixt suicide and murder."

Right!

I said,

"Me, I have endured my life between vicious cunts."

He ran the taste of that 'round his gums, then said,

"I'm not buying in to the suicide scenario."

"Why?"

He laughed, asked,

"Jesus H, how monosyllabic are you going to be?"

"A lot."

He suddenly reached down and rubbed the pup's ears, startling not only me but the pup.

The pup wasn't *buying* it.

Sheridan said,

"Here's the thing. On the ground near the fallen gun was an emerald heart."

I thought,

Oh, fuck.

He looked at me, asked,

"That mean something, partner?"

I could sink her, just drop the murderous bitch right in it.

I said,

"Not a damn thing."

He shook his head, then,

"Okeydoke, let's get to it."

I stood up, said,

"Naw, it's time you hopped on your white charger and charged the fuck off."

He stood too and was about an inch taller than me. That inch gave him a false sense of power, thinking size matters.

He said,

"You need to know I was on loan to Quantico, learned stuff about broken-down ex-cops who hit the sauce. They have a need to be recognized."

(The Quantico was a lie.)

I said,

"Like I could give a toss, no matter what kind of *super cop* you think you are. You really need to leave."

And he sat back down, said,

"I could go another shot of that there sipping whiskey."

I was torn betwixt beating him to a bloody pulp and a sneaking admiration for his sheer front. I poured him a drink, gave the pup a treat, and, ah fuck it, lit up a Red Marlboro.

He sank the drink, went,

"Ah . . ."

Said,

"Jack, me lad, we have us here a three-pronged assault."

Paused.

Asked,

"You do know what a prong is, right?"

"Any relation to a prick?"

He moved along.

Said,

"If this were a crime novel, a character who was introduced at the beginning, then seemed to be discarded, has reentered the narrative. I speak of Alexander Knox-Keaton, with all the hyphens as opposed to the trimmings. You do remember him?

He employed you as a security guard though, if you want my ten cents, you couldn't mind a flaming box of matches."

I said,

"You talk funny."

He nearly sighed, said,

"That is education, my son."

He then looked around, asked,

"Might I cadge a cig?"

I gave him one and he produced a heavy, battered gold Zippo.

Clanked that baby up and I relished the clunk of the shutting motion. Perhaps it's the pro-American in me but a Zippo has always reached a part of me that is not yet frozen.

But fuck, what does it say of a man to have his heart touched by a goddamn lighter?

I asked,

"No vaping for you?"

He snarled,

"I look like a cocksucker to you?"

"Well, yes."

I swear the pup wagged his tiny tail. He likes when I take the war to them.

He flicked ash on my worn carpet, said, all business,

"This Knox-Keaton employed you to find the notorious *Red Book* and you, major fuckhole that you are, botched the job and in walks the Mickey Mouse gang, the so-called Ghosts of Galway."

Paused.

"Wimps of Galway more like but, hey, they got lucky and found the rogue priest, offed the poor fucker then—who knew?—your *bird*."

(Bird. How'd we get back to the sixties?)

Continued.

"Emerald or some such dumb-ass jewel name, fucks the head Ghost honcho and her sidekick."

He pulled out a black notebook, checked,

"Yeah Hayden. Jesus H, where do they get these names? What happened to Paddy and Mary for chrissakes?"

He snapped his fingers, near spat,

"Gimme another smoke."

I gave him the look, said,

"Give me the bottom line on what it is you want."

He made a show of draining his glass, then,

"So Hayden for some bizarre reason gives you the book and what do you do?"

He makes a sweeping gesture with his hands, says,

"You just *hand* it on over to a nicotine priest."

With a hint of admiration, I say,

"You are well informed."

He reached into his jacket. A gun?

No.

Pack of soft-pack Camels, shucked one out, fired up.

I said,

"No thank you."

He grimaced, began,

"Your hyphened Mr. Knox was using the Ghosts of Galway to hide his real outfit, the Fenians. Like the Internet hides the dark web, these boyos are hidden by the Mickey Mouse Ghosts. These are hard-core, ex-soldiers who served in Jordan, in Syria, and under Knox they aim to launch a second Reformation."

I said,

"That's fucked up."

"No,"

He said.

"That is terrorism."

He stood up, said,

"You are going to trap Knox for us."

"Why would I do that?"

He gave a grin of such utter malice, then,

"Because I am going to let your little psycho bitch slide."

Fuck.

I near whined,

"Why would I want to save her?"

He smirked, said,

"Look at you, elderly drunken fool besotted with a hot young vixen."

As he went, he threw,

"Sew Knox up ASAP."

SWAN SONG

A swan sings only once in its life.
Just before it dies.

They

Killed

The pup.

Left his tiny heart on a bloody piece of parchment.
A note saying,
Do not fuck with the Fenians.

I was on my knees, vomiting and cradling the tiny crushed body.

Tears rolled down my battered face and mingled with the blood in his coat.

I screamed,

"I will wreak a fucking biblical vengeance on all of you."

On the parchment were block capitals:

WE—here they placed his little heart—IRELAND

Later, I was wrapping his small body in his Galway United favorite comfort shirt when the doorbell shrilled. I grabbed my hurley, flung open the door

To

Doc,

My neighbor,

Who said,

"Great news, we have a place for you on the team to Everest."

Everest!

Before I could reply, he glanced nervously at the hurley, asked,

"Everything all right, Jack?"

I near spat,

"Hunky fucking dory."

He stepped back,

Wisely, I think.

Tried,

"Perhaps I could take the wee pup for a run?"

The world tilted, and for a second I blanked out, then,

I said,

"Not really. His heart wouldn't be in it."

Shut the door with a gentle push, the violence ebbing away.

Later, not sure it was days or hours, I buried the pup in Claddagh. Near the swans. Perhaps he could hear them glide and, in a perverse way, I wanted to believe they would stand vigil for him.

I stood over the tiny grave, laid his favorite Galway United scarf on it and his now never to be eaten

Treats.

Oh, sweet Jesus.

A fellah passing, asked,

"You burying the wife?"

It was too early to kick the living daylights out of him, so I said,

"'Tis a dog."

Bitterly he said,

"Same thing."

They say if you are planning revenge
Dig two graves
If Jack was asked
He'd say
"Dig me a whole graveyard."

Alexander

Knox

-Keaton

My former boss, the man who so badly wanted to procure *The Red Book* and, according to Sheridan, the power behind the Fenians. His house was truly a mansion with a stunning view of Galway Bay. Usually two bodyguards sat outside in a BMW.

I used whatever juice I had to buy a shotgun. I wanted something

Loud

And

Nasty.

Sawed off the barrel and stashed it inside the shoplifter pocket in my all-weather Garda coat. I also took along a vicious long-bladed knife honed in the Aran Islands. I believe knives are a coward's choice and require a particular psycho set of reference.

Man, I could do fucking psycho.

As I was leaving my apartment I checked to see if there was water in the pup's bowl.

No bowl.

No pup.

No cry.

Knox-Keaton's magnificent house was not unlike a Dalí nightmare. Two built bodyguards sat outside in the BMW. I arrived at the witching hour when they were nodding off. Like a good ex-Guard I had the finest burglar's kit and was in jig time, saw the huge tapestry of *The Book of Kells*, and took my knife to it.

Sheer vandalism?

You fucking betcha.

I found the master bedroom on the second floor, mainly by following the aroma of pot and incense.

The room was dark and two people were in a deep sleep, not surprising if you factored in the empty champagne bottles and general air of debauchery. I know that gig. I've played it, if not in recent years then certainly in false memory. I cocked the shotgun, saw the woman, who appeared to be Thai, a relatively new feature on the Irish rich scene: buy yourself a girl from the poorer countries.

I nudged her with the gun, said,

"Lock yourself in the bathroom."

No argument.

Smart girl.

He was coming around with many a groan and fart. He started to rise and I said,

"Don't get up on my account."

Shoved the barrel right in his enormous gut, said,

"While you fucked, my pup burned."

No denial.

This, in semi-whine:

"I told them not to, said it was a bad idea."

I said,

"Very bad fucking idea."

He said, like a caricature of all the bad guys in bad movies,

"I have money."

I asked very, very quietly,

"Will you buy me a new pup?"

The eagerness.

"Of course, a whole litter if you want."

I smashed his nose with the butt of the shotgun.

Asked,

"Give me the names of the top Fenian guys."

He did.

Frank Cass.

Joe Tyrone.

Said they hung out at the Green Harp pub.

How fucking Fenian could you get?

I said,

"I so desperately want to kill you."

He was throwing up, so not so sure he heard me. For form's sake, I cracked his skull with the gun barrel.

Before I left I pissed long and powerfully on his Persian rug as he had pissed all over my small life.

I moved away from the area fast and was just crossing the road at Nile Lodge when a car came out of nowhere and bounced me to the far curb.

As I tumbled in the dirt, I managed to catch a glimpse of the car.

The color!

Emerald.

When
You
Have
Seen
One
Ghost
Further
Impact
Is
Muted

A combination of concussion,

Shock,

Trauma

Left me in a semi-coma

For weeks.

I missed

Brexit,

Ireland's superb performance in the Euros, even beating Italy and giving us a new football hero

Robbie Brady,

And the unique sight of Roy Keane with a smile.

Wales nearly made it to the semis.

England crashed out of both Europe in football and membership in one week.

The instigators of Brexit,

The nasty duo of Johnson and Farage, did the unthinkable:

Fucked off.

Yup, resigned.

My unconscious reeled in the maelstrom of madness.

. . . dark hounds of heaven snarling at my limping feet, to David Bowie ascending to heaven through Ridge being shot in slow motion and the faceless Woody crooning "Send in the Ghosts," *to water charges in red dripping neon leading to me screaming out the names of*

Cass

And

Tyrone,

The Fenian leaders.

Finally roaring out of it all with a gasp and a whimper.

Em was sitting by the bed, humming.

Was it

"Stairway to Heaven"?

Never no fucking mind.

She was dressed all in black.

Mourning?

Not if leather trousers,

Black Harley T-shirt,

And black Doc Martens

Are a new trend for grief.

She said,

"You had us a wee bit worried my bairn."

Scottish accent?

Then, in down-home Louisiana,

"Chet, you done gone cause us all a whole heap of worrying."

Fuck.

I asked,

"Why am I in a private room?"

Odd question?

Not in Ireland where lying on a trolley for three days is considered fortunate.

She said,

"Last time you were here I had to blow a doctor, remember?"

My head hurt.

I tried,

"This time?"

She displayed a huge ring on her finger, big diamond so authentic it had to be fake, said,

"Me and Dr. Ray Crosby are engaged."

She managed to inject *engaged* with a lurid overtone.

I asked,

"You drive an emerald-colored car?"

Giggles.

And fuck again.

She said,

"I figured you'd come after me because of the dyke cop."

I snapped,

"Sergeant Ridge was her name."

She shrugged and, I have to admit, despite my very precarious state, I couldn't help but admire the radiance, however blighted, that emanated from her. Said,

"That cunt, yeah, so I felt, despite my love for you, that I might have to, um *retaliate* first."

I sank back in the bed.

And she was over, brushed my cheek with her hand, cooed,

"Ah, heart mine, I didn't drive the car. Does that help at all?"

I snarled,

"Give me a cigarette."

I knew she'd have some. She always had the things that hurt. She lit me up.

I blew smoke at her.

She continued.

"Me and Hayden . . . you remember the kid who brought you *The Red Book*?

Stopped.

Mimed a flashbulb over her head, said,

"Don't recall a whole lot of gratitude for that hombre!"

And punched me on the arm.

"We asked the dice, *Kill the Jackster or no?*"

I looked for a place to extinguish the cig, dropped it in a glass of water, the sort of thing that annoys the shit out of me in truth.

I said,

"Lemme guess? The dice said yes."

She made a sad face, said,

"Hayden insisted he do the deed but, you know, fucked it up."

I sneered,

"Because I lived?"

She looked like she would play punch me again and I moved away from her, not easy when an IV is trailing you like bad news. She said,

"Silly you! Because the car was dented. Don't you just *hate* that?"

I said,

"Go away, just fuck off and disappear."

She was about to reply when a nurse came bustling in.

All starched uniform and biz, immediately began fluffing the pillows. They do that as a mere act of irritation, especially when you just got them nice and comfy. Em said,

"I want to be you when I'm old enough."

The nurse looked at her with a mix of incredulity and scorn, said,

"Ah, you're already too old and aren't you a teensy bit past it?"

Pause.

"For trying to rock that whole biker chick gig?"

Emily was silent as she considered her position, then asked,

"Is it difficult being gay and a nurse or do people not give a shit anymore?"

The nurse smiled, then looked at her watch, said,

"Time to go child, surely the asylum has strict curfew?"

Emily walked right over to me and, in a snap, French kissed me with a lot of heavy noise then turned, headed for the door, slapped the nurse on the bum, said,

"Keep it buttoned, Ratched."

The charities in Ireland
Prove
You can
Pretty much
Con
Most of the people
Almost all of the time.

The day of my release from the hospital I was sitting by the bed when the nurse came in, handed over a large bag, said,

"Your daughter left fresh clothes for you."

Emily.

I opened the bag carefully. She was quite capable of planting an incendiary there.

Nope.

Just clothes.

Very expensive ones.

A shirt handmade on the Aran Islands. Those suckers last for a hundred years. I, on the other hand, might be good for six months. Armani jeans, I shit thee not. But not those horrors, skinny jeans. The greatest codswallop ever apart from Irish sunglasses.

Doc Marten boots, and don't ask me how but nicely scuffed. And a pea jacket from Gap.

There was a note.

With Emily, there is always a note.

Read,

"Darlin'

Here be some clobber for the life you should have led. Cost me 1,500 euros so I went on shoplifting spree."

Then in blatant capitals:

"WHY

Did you not tell me they killed that beautiful pup?

I will spread a wrath of fucking epic dimension on the cunts who did it."

Then, in italics,

"*I swear Rhett that I will rebuild Tara.*"

She signed off with many hearts and dancing ponies.

I guess she liked them.

Least the ones who dance.

A doctor came in, clipboard at the ready and a brisk attitude they instill in med school that translates as

"You, the patient, know sweet fuck all. I, the doctor, am omnipotent."

He said,

"I am Doctor Singh."

Waited.

I looked at him; he seemed about twelve. I said,

"You inject that with a certain amount of gravitas, as if I should go, *Dr. Singh!*"

I let the length of a bad cigarette pass, then added,

"Don't mean shit to me pal."

When you have been declared at death's door and given a limited time to live by *doctors,* it tends to obliterate any lingering genetic fear you may have had.

He was stunned, mustered,

"I don't think there is any call for that."

I gave him my rabid smile, said,

"No call for Brexit, either, but here we are."

He shook his head, began to consult his file, said,

"Mr. Taylor, you have a rather colorful, checkered medical history and—"

I held up my hand, said,

"If you have a prescription for heavy-duty painkillers then we can chat but, otherwise, sayonara."

I was outside the hospital and cadged a cig from a poor creature trailing an IV.

He gave me a Major, the heavy-duty Irish cigs that would fell an ox. He looked so bad, I had to look away. I wondered if he would last the time it took me to smoke the cig. He rasped,

"We are not allowed to smoke here."

As we both fumed away.

I said,

"What will they do? Kill us?"

And, oh, fuck, instantly could have bit my tongue off. He caught it, said,

"They've already done for me in there."

Indicating the hospital. A security guard did make a brief appearance but something in my face turned him in another direction. The man said, peering at me closely,

"You're the young Taylor lad."

Lad!

We both smiled at that and he said,

"They call me *Oats.*"

I asked,

"As in *the sowing of*?"

He seemed confused, then said,

"I was the clerk for the commissioner of oaths."

Before I could comment on this he pointed a shaking finger toward the gate, said,

"I think that young girl is waving at you."

Indeed.

Dressed in what appeared to be a school uniform, she was gesturing wildly. I stubbed out the cig, said,

"Take care."

He gripped my arm, nigh pleaded,

"Will you say a few words at my funeral?"

Fuck.

"I am . . . Sure. Anything special you'd like mentioned?"

"Say about my love of hurling."

I asked,

"Love it, do you?"

He spat to his right, muttered,

"I fucking loathe it."

The girl looked familiar. She was in a school uniform but pinked up, as in chains along the blazer and a ripped seam to the side of the skirt. Then I recalled her, with a sinking feeling.

Lorna Dunphy, who had tried to employ me to find her non-existent brother. I had tracked down her dad and, oh, fuck, bad.

A broken man whose wife had committed suicide, I had drunk some Jay with him, smoked some cigs, and provided him with comfort not at all.

And suddenly I was enraged.

All these lunatics in my life. She began,

"Why haven't you found my brother? I paid you."

I took a deep breath, said,

"You don't have a brother. Stop this mad talk and . . ."

I paused,

Trying to rein in my bile,

Continued.

"And for God's sake, take the crazy pills and stop annoying people."

Like I said,

Reining it in.

She reeled back as if I had slapped her.

Did I relent?

Did I fuck.

Shouted,

"Go back to school and give up bothering people with your silly nonsense."

She turned and fled.

I muttered,

"Thank God for tact."

While this shameful episode was ensuing, Em was putting a bullet in a man's head. Two, actually, but who's counting?

“When anyone asks me
About the Irish character,
I say,
Look at the trees:
Maimed, stark and misshapen
But
Ferociously tenacious.”

(Edna O’Brien)

Frank Cass, one of the Fenians, was shot dead outside his home in Mervue. Among his possessions, the Guards found a letter threatening his life and signed by Jeremy Cooper.

The gun used in the shooting was found in Cooper's bedroom.

Slam dunk.

I heard about this and knew it was a frame and the most likely person was Emily. It was the kind of neat package she specialized in. I got a call from his solicitor, asking if I would come and see Cooper. I said,

"Seeing as how it went so well on our last meeting?"

The solicitor chuckled, said,

"Despite everything, he has a certain respect for you."

I went, mostly out of curiosity. The Guards were jubilant, told me,

"He is fucked."

I asked,

"That a legal term?"

Got the look.

Cooper seemed to have shriveled, his whole frame sunk in on itself. Too, he looked ill. Very.

He raised a limp hand, said,

"Thank you for coming."

I nodded, took the chair opposite where he was perched. I said,

"You seem to be rightly screwed this time."

He smiled and it seemed as if the very act hurt his face. He asked,

"Did you set me up?"

I said,

"No."

He continued to stare at me, then,

"I believe you; it seems a little too clever for your limited abilities."

I said,

"You seem remarkably calm for a guy in your position."

He shrugged, said,

"My health is so walloped that I won't be around for a trial."

I made to leave, he asked,

"Aren't you curious as to who did this to me?"

Now I got to do the shrug, said,

"All you psychos getting rid of each other is actually a blessing."

He savored this, then,

"The whole deal smacks of your deranged lady friend, the lovely Emily."

Now I got to smile, said,

"Like I said, all you psychos."

He wasn't letting go, tried,

"She tried to do for you once. She won't stop."

This was beginning to get on my wick, so I said,

"Have a nice life, what remains of it."

He said,

"Hayden, her little helper, he lives at 18, Mansfield Road."

When I didn't answer, he added,

"You do know he drove that green car?"

Outside, I lit a cig and his solicitor came out, said,

"Poor bastard is done for."

A young Guard came rushing out of the station, said,

"Mr. Taylor, if you have a moment, the super would like a word?"

Good heavens.

In the past if Clancy *wanted a word*, I'd be hauled in by the scruff of my neck. I said,

"Yeah, okay."

Followed him to Clancy's office.

Seated behind a massive desk, he was in full regalia, dress uniform and three Guards ranged behind his back. They almost appeared *welcoming*.

He stood up, extended his hand, greeted,

"Jack, good to see you."

I tried,

"Um . . ."

And had nothing. He nodded to one of the three, snapped,

"Get the man a chair."

They did.

I sat.

The air of welcome, of camaraderie, threw me completely. Worse, Clancy beamed at me, a huge smile encompassing whatever passed as warmth in his chilly nature.

Creepy.

"Now, Jack, I don't know if you are aware but the new minister of justice . . ."

He paused.

To see if I knew what that was?

Continued.

"Has introduced new legislation allowing ex-Guards, retired Guards, to act as consultants, advisers to the force."

Waited

Then,

"I know you have always *regretted* having to *leave* the force."

To *leave*!

Right.

As they say in the U.S., I had my arse handed to me, kicked me the fuck out, is what happened.

Now, my heart lurched. Oh, my God, was it possible I would be a Guard again? I felt dizzy with hope. I tried to speak but felt choked. Clancy looked around at the Guards, smiled, said,

"I think we may well have made Mr. Taylor's day."

The *Mr.* should have tipped me off.

Clancy began to unfold a large sheet of parchment, said,

"Have a gander at this, see how you like it."

I moved toward the desk, my legs weak, looked down at the document, read,

As

If.

For sickness of the soul
Perhaps
A doctor of metaphysics?

Do you ever recover the one great love of your life?

Me, not really.

Anne Henderson, way back, but the intensity clung to me still. Booze eased the ache but, ofttimes, intensified it. 'Tis madness for sure. She made me feel like there might be a better version of my own self.

There wasn't.

More's the Galway pity.

Past my humiliation, my deep shame at the hands of Clancy, I was walking along the beach, dogless and lost. The beach near the army barracks is usually deserted, why I chose it. The sea was a wild thing and I debated the merits of death by water.

Clean,

Said the utter mad part of my mind.

I simply stood by the water, my mind in turmoil, when I heard,

"Jack?"

Tentative.

A woman walking toward me, carefully, as if I might be dangerous. I was but not to her.

Not then.

Do you half hope the love of your life will be old and battered like your own bitter soul?

That the years have mangled and chewed the very thing you cherished?

Yes, in the realm of rage, you half desire their ruin.

She wasn't ruined.

Not a bit.

Au contraire, as they say in literary novels.

She looked gorgeous.

Anne Henderson, once the very beat of my beating heart.

We stared at each other for a moment. The *would we,*

Wouldn't we,

Hug?

It hung there like a shy reprimand. Then she held out her hand, asked,

"Jack, how are you?"

Men and women just are not built for handshakes. I took her hand, it felt like torn hope.

I said,

"Not too bad."

Jesus. Lame or what?

I mean, what if I spit it out,

Like,

They cut the heart out of my beloved pup.

The Guards reduced me to a level of shame I didn't even know I still possess.

Oh,

And a young lady I am intrigued by tried to murder me.

And

And

And

How's that sound?

She lied, said,

"You look . . ."

Pause.

"Well."

The moment when Clancy humiliated me burned anew in my mind.

To paraphrase Macbeth,

Who knew I had so much shame in me!

She examined with that close scrutiny that Irish women excel in. Said,

"I forgive you, Jack."

Fuck me.

I wanted to scream

"Oh, really? How magnanimous of you, how have I survived all these hard years without that vital act?"

I said,

"Thank you."

Then I did that thing that people do when they are completely out of the next thought. I said,

"Nippy for the time of year."

Oh, sweet God, like a stranded Brit.

And,

She laughed.

Asked,

"I wonder if I might enlist your help?"

Christ, sure, there wasn't anything on the planet I wouldn't do for her. More's the Irished dumb ass. I said,

"Depends."

Thought,

Seriously, I said that?

Her face changed, the briefest flash of annoyance, then,

"I will pay you. I didn't expect you to work for nothing."

Before I could stop myself I blurted,

"One time I would have done it for free."

Fuck.

She shook her head as if she knew such nonsense was inevitable. I asked,

"What do you need done?"

I'd swear a slight blush rose to her face but probably the wind. In Galway, we blame the wind for most things we'd prefer to not name. She said,

"It is difficult to put into words."

I said with more than a little edge,

"Think of me as a priest."

She gave a sudden abrupt laugh, startling us both, and said,

"Good God! That is the very last thing I could think of you."

Given the toxic air that priests inhabited these days, that might even have been a compliment. She asked,

"Might we meet next Monday?"
I said,
"Sure."
Set the time for six in the evening at the Meyrick Hotel.
That time, it sneers loudly,
"This is not a date."
Eight o'clock is a date and anytime in the day is just banal. But,
Six?
Six sucks.
Not
A
(Galwayed)
Hope
Of
A
Chance.

I needed to find the remaining Fenian.

After the other Fenian had been killed he'd gone to ground. But before I could even begin the search, he found me.

I'd been to the pub and, in truth, had way more than I intended. Least I think I had the intention but, as they say, it got away from me. I had bought a drink for a very attractive woman in Garavans, amazed when she smiled at me and, fueled by drink, I had sat next to her. She was in either late forties or a very battered thirties.

I was expounding on the lack of recognition for the writer Patrick Hamilton and she said,

"I don't read."

Now, I don't, God forgive me, remember her name but, alas, I do remember my reply:

"You don't read? What the fuck is wrong with you?"

And she was gone.

I staggered home, wondering if I would fry up a big batch of sausages, then thought,

"And put two down for the pup."

To instantly realize there was no pup, no more. I had that drunken moment of utter self-pity, leaning against a wall. Managed to get it together to find my way home, opened the door, and felt a gun barrel into the back of my skull.

A voice.

"Don't do anything stupid."

My whole life I had done just that. I managed,

"Shoot me now."

Heard an intake of breath and,

"What?"

"Save me a biblical hangover."

Heard a slight chuckle.

I asked,

"Let me sit down."

And moved to the armchair.

My hangover had vanished. Guns might be the new hangover cure. The man facing me was mid-height, dark curly hair, a boxer's bruised face, and eyes so brown they verged on black.

I asked,

"You here about my TV license? I heard they were getting more proactive."

The gun was lowered to rest against his right leg. He tapped it gently against that, said,

"You're a cool one."

I stared at him. He had an ease in his bearing acquired from long experience of conflict.

He said,

"I'm Joe Tyrone."

Took me a moment, then I spat,

"The other Fenian fuck."

He said,

"Just Joe would be fine."

He had a trace of an English accent and I sneered,

"You're not even Irish."

The gun came up and he took a deep breath, said,

"You need to mind your mouth. And many of the greatest Irish patriots . . ."

Paused, then,

He intoned,

"Roger Casement

Wolfe Tone
Were
Of English birth but their very souls were Fenian."

I said,

"I don't think they were into gutting dogs."

He sighed, said,

"I have a deal to offer."

I gave him the look that said,

"Dream on sucker."

He pushed on.

"We declare a truce and I give you Clancy."

Clancy!

I said,

"Clancy?"

He allowed a small smile, said,

"He is in line to be the new police commissioner, the big prize for a cop, but he needs to be . . ."

Paused.

"Squeaky clean."

"Is he?"

Tyrone said,

"Clancy likes to portray family values, and his *strong moral code* will be much praised."

He took a large envelope out of his jacket, mused,

"What if it were shown such is not the case?"

I said,

"He'd be fucked."

"Indeed."

I stared at him, let a silence build. He was one of those who could ride a silence, so I said,

"I'm thinking you want to trade."

He made a hammer of his hand, said,

"Bingo."

My shredded hangover fought with my desire to beat the living daylights out of him but I drew a deep breath, waited. He said,

"Here's what I'm thinking. I give you these . . ."

Indicating the envelope.

"And we call it quits."

I said,

"You must believe I had very little regard for my pup."

He was about to respond then rearranged that, said,

"Wasn't me did the deed. In fact I vetoed the idea."

I gave him the look that says,

"Like, seriously?"

Even in my head, it echoed of the U.S. He asked,

"Have we a deal?"

I considered my choices and went for the brazen lie, said,

"Sure, we have a deal."

The gun was slowly eased into his jacket. He moved toward the door, said,

"I won't be seeing you, then."

I nodded.

I waited a beat until he was well gone. I circled the envelope with my fingers, wondering what revelations awaited.

There were four black-and-white prints, A4 size so there was no mistaking the players.

I felt I'd been gut punched, let out a wail of

"Oh, God, no."

Never made it to the bathroom before I threw up.

Violently.

I sank down on the carpet, muttering,

"Sweet Jesus."

A pity plea or a prayer?

Does it even matter?

If the past
Is
Another country
Why
Am
I
Held
At the border?

To come cap in hand!

In Ireland, that translates as

Begging,

With a suitable amount of groveling and humiliation.

As a nation, we know it all too well.

I said the words aloud as I prepared to meet Anne Henderson.

At the mediocre time of six o'clock.

The time that says,

"You don't really count."

In many ways, it was always six o'clock in my life.

'Tis sad but true.

I wore a crisp white shirt with a tie I nicked off a Rotary bollix. My newish 501s, and the scuffed Doc Martens. You never knew when you might need to kick someone in the face.

My Garda jacket, and if I had any cologne I'd have splashed that liberally but, lacking it, I would just have to rely on my old-school charm.

Emphasis on *old*.

I headed to the Meryck Hotel to meet the former love of my life and is there a sadder sentence than that? There was no rain but the air was heavy, oppressive. The doorman at the hotel, greeted,

"Well, well, the bold Jack Taylor!"

I said,

"At least you didn't say you heard I was dead."

Which was more than a frequent greeting. He looked slightly abashed, said,

"I did hear that but I didn't like to say for fear it isn't true."

If that statement makes sense to you, you officially have an Irish mentality.

I took a seat at the rear of the hotel and waited. She arrived suitably late, dressed, if not to impress, then at least to warrant notice. Light navy raincoat over white sweater and blue jeans, flat-soled shoes.

I didn't merit heels.

She went to bestow one of those air kisses on me and I snapped,

"Seriously?"

She sat with a very small sigh. Like,

"If I had a euro for every cranky man."

She said,

"You look well, Jack."

I didn't return the compliment, asked,

"Are you familiar with the expression *cap in hand*?"

Stopped her.

Then her face got that peevish expression that screams,

"The fuck is it now?"

She said,

"Jack, I never understood half of what you were muttering about."

Muttering!

Nice.

I said,

"Thanks for feeling you could share that but, back to the topic, it means to beg."

She threw her hands up, said,

"Whatever."

I gave her my second best smile, the one that is driven by malice.

I said,

"You never thought much of my work as an investigator."

She didn't leap in, protesting, in fact she said nothing.

The old silent assention.

Never no mind.

I continued in a very quiet, almost soothing tone,

"But what if I know what you want to tell me and . . ."

Big dramatic pause.

"Might even have the actual help you wish to get?"

She was stunned but disbelieving.

Said,

"I think that would be highly unlikely."

The waitress came, adding to the nice air of tension, building mightily.

I ordered a Jameson, and Anne, almost desperately, a vodka and slimline tonic.

She went to ask me something and, very annoyingly, I made the shush gesture, let the drinks arrive.

They did.

And she gulped down the vodka without the tonic, slimline or otherwise. I said, *sipping* at my Jay,

"The rehab centers say more and more women are showing up. They call it the wine factor or indeed perhaps the *whine* factor."

She was not amused, snapped,

"Get to it."

I said,

"You were sleeping with Superintendent Clancy, photos were taken, and said photos now jeopardize his chance to become the police commissioner."

She was stunned.

I asked,

"Did I miss anything? He sure has a fat arse."

She did that new gig, *crying without tears*. You see it on reality TV. She whispered something I couldn't decipher but I guess it wasn't *So sorry, Jack.*

I asked,

"Is that you saying amazing job?"

She sniffled some more, then,

"What do I have to do?"

I could have been nasty, said,

"A blow job for openers."

I did say,

"Nothing, nothing at all."

She grasped at this tiny straw, said,

"Oh, Jack, thank you."

I let that false gratitude hover a wee while, then,

"But Clancy, he has to do something."

Suspicious,

And more than a little angry, she asked,

"What had you in mind?"

I said,

"To come to me, cap in hand."

I prompted,

"You do recall at the beginning of our tête-à-tête I explained that expression?"

She gave a deep sigh, eerily reminiscent of my late mother and, God knows, that bitch could sigh for Ireland. She said,

"What does that actually mean in this case?"

I gave her a warm smile, no real warmth but lots of patience. I said,

"He puts on his dress uniform, comes to my door, knocks . . ."

I paused and, very annoyingly, made the gesture of knocking.

Continued.

"Then he whips off his ceremonial hat and, bingo, done deal."

She stood up, adjusted her coat, gave me a tight cold smile, asked,

"Anything else?"

I acted like I gave it some serious consideration, said,

"Tell him to grovel a little."

"It's not that the Irish
Are cynical.
It's simply that they have a wonderful
Lack of respect
For everything and everybody."

(Brendan Behan)

Clancy waited two days before he showed up. Early evening, a short knock at my door.

Solid, authoritative.

I let him simmer then opened the door. He wasn't in uniform. I gave him a look of perplexity, asked,

"Help you?"

He gave a grunt of barely suppressed rage, said,

"Not a time for your usual bullshit."

And brushed past me.

I weighed my options:

Scream obscenities,

Throw him out,

Shoot him?

Much as I liked the third one, I closed the door, said,

"How have you been?"

Let a beat pass, then,

"Tom?"

He was checking out the room, seeing nothing to impress him. He said, gritted teeth,

"I, um, appreciate you doing this, Jack."

I shut the door, walked carefully to the chair, sat opposite him, the coffee table between us, and thirty years of bile. I said, with great warmth,

"Glad to be of help."

And I sat still.

He glanced around, definitely on edge, tried,

"If ever there is anything you need, some *special* assistance with?"

I let that hum, then asked,

"Like if I hadn't paid my TV license?"

He gave a tight smile, said,

"Always the smart mouth but, really, if you get in a bind?"

Bind!

I said,

"Bind? Hell of a word."

Enough fencing.

I reached behind me, produced a large brown envelope, laid it flat on the table. He stared at it, tried,

"Thing between me and Anne, it was simply a fuck and run."

I bit my lip, managed not to smash his face, said,

"There you go and . . . off you go."

He stood, contemplated a hand shake, settled for

"Thanks again."

And was gone.

Clancy was in his office, the envelope before him. He had shut his door, barked at his secretary,

"No calls."

He let out a sigh of relief, couldn't believe it had been so easy. He picked up a gold letter opener, presented to him by the Rotary Club, sliced the top of the package.

Went,

"Huh?"

As he pulled out large blank sheets of paper.

In the middle was a page with black capital letters.

Took him a moment then he read

AS

IF.

For once, I did the right thing.

I mailed the photos to Anne. I didn't want to. In truth I wanted to wound her but I ignored the base instinct and sent them. There was the bonus of Clancy not sending his thugs to collect them from me. After I left the post office I paused to take a moment. A bedraggled busker was hammering

"Galway Girl"

So badly, as if he had a mission to ruin Steve Earle's song. I walked past him and he muttered,

"Call yerself a patron of the arts?"

I couldn't think of a witty rejoinder so I gave him ten euros. He looked at it, said,

"Great, I can now retire."

When buskers on the street abuse you, after you gave them money, something is seriously fucked.

I got back to the apartment and immediately knew there was someone inside. Not that I am psychic but loud music was playing. Sounded like Status Quo. I eased the door open and saw Emily dancing in the middle of the room, singing along with Quo. Trust me, to sing along with them is a feat of dark madness. I found the source, a small player on the bookshelf, turned it off. Emily stood mid–dance step, went,

"You're not down with the headbangers?"

I didn't even know what that meant, asked,

"Why are people constantly breaking into my home?"

She giggled, yeah, giggled! Said,

"Because we love you, Jack-o."

She was dressed in black jeans, white T, and her hair was brightest blond. The whole outfit gave her an almost *waif* appearance, which might have been appealing if she wasn't so flat-out crazy. She flopped into a chair, drew a silver flask from her bag, drank deep, did a mock shudder, gasped.

"Fuck, that *is* good."

Then looked at me, offered the flask, which I declined. She said,

"Jack me boy, we have us a

Quandary,
Quagmire.

Laughed.

Added,

"Well, all sorts of shite beginning with a Q."

I waited.

She let out a deep dramatic sigh, said,

"One of us has to go."

I asked,

"I'm thinking it's not you?"

She did a tiny two-step shuffle, said,

"Exactly. And, logically, I'm prettier and younger, well, just about everyone is younger than you now, save for Bruce Springsteen."

I asked,

"Where might you suggest I *go*?"

She seemed to give it some serious thought, then,

"I'm hearing Honduras is lovely this time of year."

I nearly laughed.

I gave her a long hard stare but she merely smiled back. I asked,

"And if I don't?"

She did a little jig, spun 'round to face me, said,

"Then, it's party time."

I said,

"There is a super cop, some kind of Special Branch guy named Sheridan, who is gunning for you."

She echoed,

"*Gunning*?"

Then,

"How very you."

She stretched and, I think but I'm not sure, yawned, said,

"I'm off and will see you on . . ."
Searched for a description, got
"The road to happy destiny!"
As she reached the door, I said,
"I have one major advantage."
She asked,
"Pray tell?"
"I don't give a fuck."

If the ghost of your dead father
Comes to you,
It is a sign of good things.
If your dead mother comes to you,
Get a Mass said.
No,
Get many said.

Doc.

I hadn't seen him since the pup was killed. I knew his climb of Everest was due very soon. We had once been fairly tight but Emily got in the middle and screwed that.

When he did knock on my door, I wasn't entirely sure how to respond. He asked,

"May I come in?"

I nearly said no. He looked like a down-and-out and his eyes had that bleak despair I had sometimes witnessed in the mirror. I said,

"Okay."

He had an air of being dazed and his clothes were shabby. This was a guy who always turned out neat and polished. He glanced around the room, asked,

"Where's the pup?"

Fuck.

I said,

"He ran off."

He had no reply to this bare statement.

Asked,

"Could I get a drink?"

I made him work for it, asked,

"Tea, coffee, or a cool bottle of Galway water?"

I could see the pain in his face and thought,

"Yeah, payback's a bitch."

He near cried,

"Something with a kick?"

The temptation to snap,

"Like a twelve-gauge?"

Instead I got the Jameson, poured him a fine wallop, handed it to him. His hand shook like a withered prayer. He asked,

"You not having one?"

Twenty years I waited to say this,

"Bit early for me."

Oh, the jolt of self-righteousness.

Divine.

He tried not to gulp it but failed and stared into the bottom of the now empty glass. I could have told him there was nothing there even if I still looked into that emptiness every empty day. He said,

"Whoever took my laptop got into my online banking and cleaned me out."

I said, trying not to inject too much granite in my tone,

"If I recall you told the Guards it was me."

It was like a lash in his face and his head dipped but I was far from finished, I added,

"Least we both know that level of expertise is beyond me."

He said,

"I'm sorry, Jack."

Bit late.

I asked,

"So what do you want?"

In as harsh a sound as that echoes.

He stood up, as if that would help, asked,

"I hate to do this but could you lend me some money?"

Before I could answer, he added,

"I'd pay you back, even add interest."

I said,

"I could maybe go a hundred."

He stared at me for a long minute then gave a harsh bitter laugh, said,

"A hundred? A fucking hundred? Are you kidding me? What the fuck would that do? Wouldn't pay for one fucking day."

I felt a vague string of rage, not spitting but there. I asked,

"What sort of figure had you in mind?"

He was near trembling with,

With,

Indignation?

He said,

"About ten grand."

I took a deep breath, said,

"Maybe I should be flattered that you believe I have that kind of dough."

Dough.

Well, I was a bit thrown. I tried,

"Sorry."

He looked at me like *sorry* was the last fucking thing he wanted to hear, said,

"You know people."

What did that even mean?

I asked,

"What does that even mean?"

He snarled.

"Don't play fucking coy."

I tried,

"You think some of the hotshots I have dealt with would give me the bloody time of day?"

He gave a slightly sinister grin, said,

"You have information on a lot of them."

The whole experience was so bizarre that it took me a moment to grasp the implication, then I near shouted,

"Blackmail?"

For the very first time his English accent emerged fully as he said,

"You *Paddies* like to soft soap things, so let's say *persuade*."

Before I could savage him, he was on his feet, said,

"Don't go anywhere, I have something."

He rushed from my place, across the corridor, and spent about five minutes in his apartment, then back, clutching a large ornate box, put it on the table, opened it, and said,

"Voilà."

Not sure what I expected but *dueling pistols*?

I asked,

"You're challenging me to a duel?"

He nearly smiled, said,

"Those date back to the Crimean War and have been in our family for generations. Not only are they oiled and clean but . . ."

He paused for the final flourish.

"Fully loaded."

Seeing my look of utter confusion, he said,

"Pull back the hammer and boom."

That was clear enough but what wasn't was why he had them on my coffee table. He said,

"Sell them."

For fuck's sake.

"To who, whom?"

He hadn't completely thought it through but tried,

"Collectors."

"In Galway, seriously?"

He checked his watch, asked,

"Do you have a train timetable?"

I was way out of patience, said,

"Check your phone."

"That's gone, like everything."

Then he turned and was gone.

“In Irish folklore are two
Dueling ghosts.
The victor is returned to life.
The vanquished is left to melancholy haunting.”

(De Brun, *Irish Folklore*)

Sometimes, for no rhyme or reason, we get a beautiful fine day, the sun just splitting the Galway rocks. It made us quite silly. We threw coats and caution to the West of Ireland wind.

Ice cream trucks rushed out of storage and made a rapid killing. Men in shorts, sandals with thick socks paraded their booty with élan. The shocking events of Syria, the Irish Olympic ticket scandal, the 13 billion that Apple owed us in tax all took a breather. Were we bathing in one day of delusion?

You fucking betcha.

I was sitting outside Garavans, a pint before me and my mind in a state of blank verse. I heard something whistle at turbo speed through my hair and then the large window behind me shattered. Way too late to duck, I muttered,

"God almighty."

My phone buzzed, put it to my ear, heard Em say,

"Shite, missed."

A beat, then,

"Your turn."

A man behind me said,

"Freak accident."

I didn't say what I knew. A high-velocity bullet.

So she was indeed deadly serious about a *duel* and then I thought,

"Well, I do *have* dueling pistols."

* * *

The world was in some dire strait. Trump seemed within an insult of the White House. Aleppo was being bombed mercilessly and a presidential candidate asked,

"What's Aleppo?"

At home, a respected [*sic*] father of three children murdered them and his wife

With

A hammer

And

His hands.

Then the piece of shit left a letter arranging how the Guards were to be contacted.

Think that's bad?

Many papers eulogized him as a

Great

Teacher,

Father,

Community organizer,

Sportsman,

And a guard of honor lined up as his coffin was brought in to the church.

Words fail me.

Mayo and Dublin were in the All-Ireland hurling final. Mayo hoped to finally lay its *curse* to rest.

What curse?

In 1951, Mayo won the All-Ireland and, returning home to the West in a victorious coach, they did not stop to allow a funeral to pass. The priest (them being the still glory days for the clergy) cursed them, uttering,

"Ye will *never* win another All-Ireland."

Only in Ireland.

Nor had they won since.

As I approached my apartment, I wondered what fresh hell awaited me there. Of course my heart sank each time I realized the pup would not be greeting me with his wild and fierce welcome. I swallowed hard as I forced that image from my mind. I opened the door carefully and very slowly, of all the sights I could have envisaged, I never would have hit on what I now saw.

A dragon.

A green carving in balsam wood.

How do I know balsam? It said so on the dragon's tail. It was about three feet in height and two in length. Truth to tell, it was a stunning piece of work. More impressive, a nigh perfect depiction of a girl on the creature's back. Beside it was a green envelope. I opened it to find many pages of a letter.

Began thus:

> Mon amour Jacques
>
> Mea culpa for resorting to the ancient art of missive communication. Social media is so

2015. As you read, you will notice many accents and as you can be dense I will alert you as they pop up. Currently, I am utilizing a BBC quite posh one so do feel suitably inferior.

That is, after all, the point of accents. If you doubt this, listen to Boris Johnson.

Too, you will see rather than hear laughter, as in,

Ha ha.

Personally, I never found laughter in written form as the slightest bit amusing. There are many cinema references buried in the letter for your entertainment plus, of course, literary allusion. The main *thrust* of this missive is to GET YOUR FUCKING ATTENTION.

I, as they say, fired the first salvo and you seem oddly reluctant to engage.

But you will.

I feel your focus waning even as you read so here is a shot of adrenaline.

Will I kill the nun?

Ha ha.

I put the letter down, rage and disbelief fighting for ascendancy. I moved over to the cupboard, took out the Jay, and fast hammered a double shot. Felt it hit like worry and then

The artificial calm. Breathe in and out, then resumed the letter of insanity.

"Did you have to go and grab a drink, Jack-o?"

It was eerie and downright spooky how she could predict my responses.

I read on.

Search la femme and I will admit, the nun, Maeve? She was the very soul of hospitality but, truly, a silly bitch. She bought every line of bullshit I trotted out. I nearly offed her there and then and, get this, you'll laugh (if not yer actual *ha ha*), she gave me a rosary. You think it would be ironically religious if I strangled her with them there beads (South Carolina accent here; pay attention!)?

Would killing a nun merit a special fire in hell and, make no mistake, mister, you and me are hell-bent. I love you Jack, moi coeur, but you have become a distraction and, let's be honest, a tiny bit boring and, while we're deep sharing here, fellah, what is the fucking deal with the dogs? I mean seriously? To lose one, okay, no harm, no foul, and tragic and all that good shite, but two, c'mon, what's that about?

Deep sigh here my alky friend, can you hear it, like a cry dredged up from the pit of an emerald soul. I gotta fly so get your fucking act together and do *something.* Don't be a whiny arse all your wasted life. One last memo afore I go. You look at the green dragon and listen up! It's Emerald you stupid bollix.

Yours in infamy,

Em.

Xxxxxxxxxx

P.S. Did you get the lit references to
Joyce,
Kafka,
Rilke,
South Park?

The difference between
A ghost
And
A banshee
Is
Seeing a ghost is literally
A scare;
Seeing a banshee
Is death.

Sister Maeve had been in my life for over a decade. And, oddly enough, we hadn't become enemies. She had once enlisted my help in Church matters and per usual I muddled through, not doing a whole lot but not really causing a whole lot of damage, either. She was the outreach for the Poor Clares and if she were the face of a new church, it might yet survive. She had a sweet tooth and loved few things more than Black Forest gâteau. I liked her a lot.

En route to warn her about Emily, I stopped at Griffin's Bakery, which specialized in a wonderful bread called the grinder. Sounds like a euphemism for Trump, who had been mercilessly skewed by the brilliant Alec Baldwin on *SNL*. A line had already formed for grinders.

Such was their word-of-mouth fame.

I thought about the perfect pint:

Hold the glass at 45-degree angle
            Pour slowly
To halfway
Stop
Go for a smoke
Return and fill
Let sit
For the head to form
Voilà!

The papers screamed not of

Aleppo,

Or

Trump,

Or even

The looming Guards strike.

No.

Kim flaming Kardashian.

You believe it?

Robbed, bound and gagged, in her exclusive Paris apartment.

Of ten million in jewels.

Her bodyguard was away in a nightclub. Whatever else you thought about clan Kardashian and, God knows, one tried to think nothing at all, you had to admit to Kim's ability to make money. Okay, so she made it by showing every bit of her bod in every possible way but, fuck, last year she made sixty-five million.

Yeah, read that and freaking weep.

If you want to know what God thinks of money, look at who he gave it to. Young girls didn't want to be Hillary Clinton (God forbid) or Katie Hopkins; they wanted the Twitter/Instagram fame of a vacuous Kardashian.

Woe is indeed fucking us.

Big time.

And I was going to visit a nun.

From
A
Kardashian
To
A
Nun.
From
A
Jack
To
A
King.
Big hit when I was a kid.
Like a bad title for a bad Lifetime Channel movie.
I walked the William Joyce route.
Infamous during the Second World War as the voice of Nazi propaganda.
Known as *Lord Haw-Haw.*
The night before the British hanged him, he wrote,
My Dear Margaret
I am anxious that you should
Go to Galway and see the docks,
Long Walk,
O'Brien's Bridge,
Nile Lodge,

Taylor's Hill,
Lenaboy Castle on the Corrib,
But, above all,
The stretch from Salthill to Blackrock
The promenade where we used to live behind.

As I reached Sister Maeve's small house I didn't realize that over the years I had

Dangerously

Recklessly

Missed the point.

But now

I had missed the play.

Mystery writers like to utilize misdirection. I had not only

Been misled but played, as British novelists say,

Like a sap.

Sister Maeve opened her door with

"Oh, the Lord sent you."

I thought,

Probably not the Lord.

She wrapped me in a warm Galway hug and, take my battered word, you have never really been hugged until a nun grabs you. Then she stood back, surveyed me, said,

"Come in and have tea."

I went into her spotless living room, and she indicated the comfortable chair. I handed over a box of Black Forest and a bottle of Baileys and she literally cooed with delight, though protesting,

"You shouldn't have, you lovely man."

Me and *lovely* have rarely inhabited the same sentence. She opened the Black Forest box and swooned.

"These are a wicked temptation."

She made tea and put the treats on a dainty plate. Then sat, looked right at me, said,

"You have a gorgeous daughter."

Fuck

Sweet

Fuck

Again.

I had come to warn her of the danger of Emily and now what?

"Oh, by the way, my *daughter* is going to kill you!"

Yeah, that would fly.

Maeve put her cup down, rose and went to the cupboard, took out a heavy large crucifix, said,

"Your girl gave me this."

There was a question lurking in there so I waited as she handed me the cross. She said,

"It is a beautiful piece but odd."

I echoed,

"Odd?"

"Yes, see how the figure of Christ is huddled to the left, leaving a space almost vacant to the right."

Indeed, the figure seemed to be almost cowering away to the left. I said,

"It is certainly . . ."

Searched for a less threatening description and gave

"Different."

Maeve had a tiny smile in play, as if she shouldn't be amused, then,

"Your girl said she wanted to leave room for you on the cross."

I had to say it, said,

"Please don't allow that *girl* . . ."

Pause.

"Into your home again."

Maeve was pouring more tea. I was sick of tea and wanted to wallop a large Jameson. Wouldn't even need the black pint as outrider. She sat down, folded her hands in that quiet manner that nuns learn at nun school, said,

"Emily has professed a wish to pursue a vocation."

Fuck.

I nearly shouted,

"As what, a clerical hit person?"

I said,

"She is seriously disturbed. She needs locking up but not in a convent."

Another thin smile, then,

"Emily said you would not react well as your love and over-protection would manifest itself."

I shook my head, stood up, said,
"Just be careful."
Maeve stood and gave me a tight hug, said,
"I have a sister."
WTF?
How was this relevant to friggin' anything?
I said, hard leaking over my tone,
"How nice!"
She tut-tutted, a pretty annoying sound in truth, then,
"She has been living in America and is now coming home."
Again, like how absolutely *fucking fascinating*.
I tried,
"Great."
Maeve still had me in a half hug, said,
"Would you like to meet her?"
Couldn't help myself, blurted
"Like, a *date*?"
I swear, she blushed, said,
"It's not good for you to be alone."
I said,
"Sure, let's do that."
Thinking hell would freeze over many Irish times before that.
As I finally made my escape, she touched my arm, said,
"There are ghosts all over this city, Jack."
What?
I said,

"What?"

She looked real sad, said,

"You have the air of a haunted man and the ghosts of the past seem to dog your steps. Please look to the light."

I nearly laughed, asked,

"The light? And where exactly would that be?"

"Oh, Jack, the light is all about you. Just ask for God's hand."

I was in Garavans in jig time, double Jay and black before me. I warned the barman,

"Don't even think of talking to me."

He muttered something like,

"Who the fuck ate your cake?"

I could have said,

"I don't do cake."

But I said nothing.

Nothing at all.

"You eat what you kill, Frank," said Lipsky.
"You never did see it. Where the power is."

(Nicholas Petrie, *The Drifter*)

"I didn't know I had permission to murder and maim."

(Leonard Cohen, on the release of his
new album *You Want It Darker*)

I went to a little-frequented pub off the docks. Not the one where I go to purchase guns but the one you go for solitude. I had a lot to be solitary about.

Emily's friend Hayden, the young kid who literally ran me over. I had his address so did I go and punch his ticket?

And when,

Fucking when?

Did I take Emily off the board my own self?

What was it that prevented me from dealing with her? It was as if she was the one friend/enemy/ally who kept me tenuously connected to life.

Makes no sense, Christ above, I know that.

As I downed my first Black pint and Jay chaser, I muttered to myself and, oh, sweet Lord, as if invoking the wrath of the fates, said this,

"What does she have to do that finally stirs me to action?"

Be real careful what you mutter. It's not always the force of light that is listening.

The pub was so far under the radar that you could light a cig and nobody gave a good fuck.

Too, this pub was infamous for its reputation for ghosts.

Yup, *ghosts.*

It was said the souls of the despaired linger on here after closing time.

To my left, wreathed in smoke, was a dark figure, putting back single brandies like time had run out.

Maybe it had.

Years ago, I had encountered an ex-exorcist in this very place and he had affected me to my very core. Peering closer, I realized with a jolt that it was the same man.

Jesus wept, and the man was staring at me, so I raised the Jameson, said,

"Slainte a match."

His face was so lined, you could plant spuds there. Not so much lived in as squatted in.

He gave a rueful smile, asked,

"Care to join me, Jack?"

I did.

Saw he had his own bottle of booze under the table, he saw me glance at it, asked,

"You ever eat Kettle crisps?"

WTF?

I said,

"I'm old school. It's Tayto for me."

That seemed to trigger a memory for him and he gave a wide smile. The change made him look like a warm, compassionate human being. He said,

"Reason I ask is the owner of said crisps sold the company for a zillion dollars and then he produced his own vodka, made purely from the humble spud, and it won the best vodka of the year 2015. It is so pure you don't get a hangover."

I seriously doubted that but what the hell, if it worked for him!

He said,

"Called Chase."

I said, without thinking,

"As in, *cut to the*?"

Again that smile.

I said,

"I'm sorry but I forgot your name."

Dark cloud danced across his eyes. He near spat,

"Legion."

Then he not so much smiled as grimaced. There was something way off about him. Previously, though I remembered him as deeply wounded, truly damaged, there was a warmth in him, made all the more appealing by his very shattered heart.

Now, he reeked of a sly maliciousness, a meanness that lit his mouth like a nasty knife gash.

He said,

"Here, they call me Jacob or . . ."

And here he tittered.

(If you have ever heard *tittering,* then you know it is really appalling.)

Continued,

"They call me *Father* Jacob when they want to borrow money or even when . . ."

Pause.

Then snigger.

"They want a blessing."

The idea of *blessing* seemed to cause him huge mirth. What the fuck ever, I had enough, and said,

"Bhi curamach"— Be careful.

He stared right at me, said,

"I switched sides."

I didn't want to know, said,

"Right, good luck with that."

He suddenly trembled, intoned,

"You have the death of the young girls on your dirty soul."

Uttered with such ferocity that I reeled back, managed,

"One. One little girl, Serena May."

He cackled.

I got the fuck away from him. At the door I felt a whoosh of wind and turned back to see him hold up two fingers and mouth

"*Two*."

Months later, I watched the TV series based on *The Exorcist*. There is a scene where the embattled priest Marcus shouts at the demon in an old crone's body,

"I compel you in the name of Our Lord to leave this woman's body."

There is a moment as the woman is silent then the eyes flash open and a deep voice sneers,

"Do I seem compelled?"

The voice sounded eerily like Jacob.

Or, indeed, *Father* Jacob.

If

You are in need of a dark blessing.

Ghost.

The spirit or soul of a deceased person
Appearing to the living.
An apparition.
A mere semblance or shadow.
Ghost word, word having no right to existence.

In "Thunder Road" Springsteen sang of
The ghosts of all the girls
He used to know.

Ghost words, most of Jack Taylor's speech, drunk or sober.

I took the decision to rest up.

Had Vinny from Charlie Byrne's load me with books:

The Hermit, Thomas Rydahl,

The Drifter by Nicholas Petrie,

Anything by Jason Starr and Hilary Davidson.

For viewing,

I had

HBO, *The Night of*,

The Australian series,

Glitch,

The brilliant *Spotless*,

Final episode of *The Fall* for the shocking violence, which sang to the seething menace of my heart.

And of course the heresy of bottled stout,

And bottles of Jay.

Pack of Red Marlboro if the nicotine raises its alluring head,

And was all set when the doorbell rang.

Fuck

And sweet

Fuck again.

Sheridan, the super cop.

Bearing all kinds of biblical bad news.

Like this.

He was dressed in a brown duster like Kevin Costner in *Tombstone.*

Had the stones to pull it off. Black 501s in way better shape than mine, a "Granddad" sparkling white T-shirt, and those fine boots he'd sported before. Around his neck was a Cimino scarf.

Somehow I seriously doubted he walked the spiritual path. He pushed past me, said,

"Get us some booze, partner. We sure as shit are gonna need it."

I was mildly amused as opposed to homicidal, which is always a relief. I asked,

"You channeling the Old West?"

He asked,

"Like it?"

I think he meant the outfit, so I said,

"A shade Village People."

He laughed and I remembered he did that a lot yet never seemed amused. He said,

"And you, my friend, are still doing the homeless attire."

Touché.

I poured us two healthy Jays and waited.

He launched,

"Your neighbor, Doc? Took the express train from Dublin."

From?

I asked,

"*From?*"

He downed the Jay, gulped, said,

"Sorry, *under*."

WTF?

He saw my shocked face, put up his hand, cautioned,

"Whoa, don't get into the drama just yet, there's more."

I sat, shock lashing at my heart, nodded.

He said,

"That old girlfriend of yours."

Paused.

Took out a notebook, read,

"Anne Henderson?"

I hung my head in horror and he continued,

"Yeah, Annie took the long swim on the small beach beside Renmore Barracks. *Renmore?* That's how you guys pronounce it, am I right?"

He lit a cig from a soft pack of Camels, blew a near perfect ring, then said as he removed a tobacco bit from his lip,

"Here's the weird thing, Jackie. She left her clothes neatly folded on the sand with a green emerald on top."

Drew long on the cig, then,

"Probably fake. The stone I mean, you think?"

In Galway, close to the old docks,
There is, they say,
A ghostly apparition of young Celia Griffin
Who never made it to
The coffin ships
Sailing to America
To escape the famine.
She was six years old.

I went to the Protestant church and, feeling alien there, I pondered revenge.

I thought of

Anne

The pup

Doc

Ridge.

Especially Ridge.

And all the grief lashed upon my life.

I could as the Yanks say

Suck it up.

Turn the other cheek and thus be a humble and better person.

Fuck that.

I could embrace the darkness and wreak havoc *on them all.*

Later in the day, I met with a notorious psycho/arms dealer who owed me for a serious favor I had done for him years ago. I handed him two names:

Alexander Knox-Keaton,

Joe Tyrone.

I told him,

"Make them suffer first."

The others?

Oh, they required a personal touch.

* * *

I shot Hayden in the back of the head.

I went to his address at 18, Mansfield Road.

Piece of shit lock on the door and any noise I made was drowned by a crashing din from his front living room. He was sprawled on a sofa, a bong in his hand and numerous cans of special brew strewn on the floor. He was watching the video game

Mafia 3.

How'd an old goat like me know that?

I read the cover.

I stood behind him, visions of the love of my life, Anne, dead in the cold water of the Renmore inlet. I put the gun right against his skull,

Pulled the trigger.

Said

"Game over."

I used my phone to take his picture with the gem showing clearly, sent it to Emily with the text

"Game on."

Emily was waiting in my apartment, dressed like Cat Woman, a cig trailing smoke in her left hand and one of the dueling pistols in her right. She for the first time said not one word.

I picked up the other pistol, said,

"Here are the rules of the duel."

Shot her in the face.
Said,
"I lied.
        There
                Are
                    No
                        Rules."

The

Fleeting

Ghost

Of

Happiness

You'd think I would have sunk into a sodden mire of depression and guilt.

Right?

Nope.

I hit a time of utter joy and near love.

Sister Maeve's sister, home from America, contacted me,

And,

Lo and fucking behold,

She was gorgeous and lovely and all sorts of unbelievable things.

Sweet Lord above.

I was near delirious with anticipation and expectancy and the endless possibilities.

Two weeks into this,

We were having dinner in the Galleon, the sound of the Atlantic Ocean right outside the window. We were toasting our crazy new love when a man approached.

Picked up my lady's glass of red wine,

And threw it in my face.

Snarled,

"You piece of shit, what did you say to my daughter?"

I realized he was the father of Lorna Dunphy, the unbalanced girl who had harassed me to find her nonexistent brother.

He saw the recognition cross my face and then he spat in my eyes, roared,

"Yeah, my beloved angel hung herself from that tree in Barna Woods."

Call it shock but in my peripheral vision, through the plate glass window, I saw them come as if from the ocean itself.

Line

On

Line,

Silent

And accusing,

The Ghosts of . . .

I recalled the ex-exorcist priest Father Jacob, saying,

"Two girls."

His fingers held up when I looked back. His sneer above two raised fingers.

His satanic laughter echoing from Barna Woods to

The shore of Salthill.

A fitting end.